Gowie Corby Plays Chicken

FOR ALL MY BADDIES

In the morning
I wake up.
In the morning
I get up.
I go down and eat my food, and
Then I go to rotten ole school.

From Vincent
to Mrs. Kemp

Prologue

The sun shines into a large, comfortable room where a family of six, four children and two adults, is having breakfast. It is Sunday morning.

"Why, she's done it, then," exclaims the father of the family, looking up from his newspaper.

"Who's done what, Dad?" asks the oldest child, a boy.

"Rosie. My friend Rosie. Listen. This is what they've got here. Dr. Rosie Angela Lee has been nominated for the Nobel Peace Prize for her work with children in need throughout the world. . . ." He pauses. "Good old Rosie."

"That's the one who sent me that super book at Christmas," announces the youngest child, through a large quantity of jam.

"Yes, that's the one," says her mother, removing some of the jam. "Your father's first girl friend."

"Why didn't you marry her, then?" asks the stroppy one, the second.

"She wouldn't have him," says their mother.

"Well, she wouldn't have anyone else, either. But I tell you one thing."

"You're always telling us one thing, Dad," says the stroppy one, bored.

"Sh," says his mother.

"If it hadn't been for Rosie, you probably wouldn't be here now, and I would be in gaol, I suspect. . . ."

"Not you, Dad. You've always been one of the goodies. . . ."

"Little do you know. Why, come to think of it, I must have been one of the first of those kids to receive the benefit of Rosie Angela Lee."

Chapter 1

Zig zag zooligan
Zim zam bum.

I didn't want to go back but then I never do, anyway.
I can't believe that school can ever happen again after
the summer holidays, but it does, and then, there I am
right in the middle of it, and there doesn't seem to have
been anything else, ever. I feel I've always been at
school and I'll be there till I die. At this point of misery
I find a marble in my pocket and start to kick it round
the playground. It goes down a drain, of course, so I
eat up the bag of skeleton bones that I've brought for
lunch, screw up the packet and kick that around
instead. And the whistle blows so I set off for the classroom, last year's, 'cos that's where we have to go first
before we're moved on to the new one.

"Corby. Gowie Corby," shouts a voice. "Pick up that
litter."

I pick it up, hate, hate. They've started already.
Picking on me. Bossing me about. Telling me off. Gowie
Corby, Gowie Corby, the theme tune for all that's
wrong in this school. All this is ahead of me, lying in
store for me, week after week after week, being tidy,
trying hard, working, reading, writing, doing Maths,

copying down all those boring boardfuls of old crap. ~~rubbish~~

Just to think of it makes me want to lie down in the corridor, right now, and give up.

Inside the classroom, the kids are milling around, jabber, jabber like crazy. I sit on a table and contemplate my new boots with the platform soles, the beauties, and I wait. In the fullness of time we shall be told to go to the new classroom. The kids are so excited it's unbelievable. You'd think the average age was five to listen to 'em. But, eventually, we move on. To the new room, the torture room, my prison for the next year. We've got two teachers team-teaching us, Mr. Merchant, who's been here as long as I can remember, and a new one, a bird named Plum, which should be all right for a few laughs, though she's not bad for a teacher, long dark hair and less than a million years old. Merchant is all right as long as you don't put a foot wrong, then he's apt to blow, like Vesuvius, like crazy.

Coats and shoebags are to go in the cloakroom. I haven't got mine. I can't remember where they are, and I haven't got any plimsolls anyway. I can't be bothered with gym or P.E. We're told to get a tray to put our gear into. Gear I have not got, but I grab a tray next to that belonging to Jonathan Johns—call me JJ, he says—glistening and gleaming in full school uniform, brief-case crammed with equipment, pens, pencils, felt tips, rulers, rubbers, set square, compasses, clip board and bulldog clips, sellotape and paper clips. He bristles with school gear like a hedgehog. Just what is he aiming at? Mastermind, maybe? Not that I care, but it's handy to be near him, 'cos he's always got something you can knock off and it's useful to be able to pinch something of his when the teacher finds you haven't got a pen for the third day running. So there I am popping my tray next to his in the unit, when he says, right out of the blue, completely unprovoked, I hadn't said anything—

"Push off, Corby. Find some place else."

A new silver papermate is lying on top of the books in his tray, I notice.

"Well, that's nice," I say gently. "What's got into you, Jonathan? Rotten holiday?"

He doesn't respond to my friendly greeting.

"Keep your rotten maulers off my things," he says.

"What unkind words. Don't be like that, Jonathan. When have I ever touched anything of yours?"

"All the time. All the time."

"You callin' me a thief?"

"Yeh. Yeh. Somethin' like that. Somethin' like that."

Jonathan always thinks that what he says is so fantastic that he's got to say it twice in case you missed it the first time round. And what he's standin' there sayin' is a bit much, I feel. So—

"You askin' for a knuckle sandwich?" I show him my power–packed bony fist and wave my eight-inch thick-soled boots at him. He's encountered the weight of my right boot before.

"Don't lose your cool, Gowie," he says, quickly. "I was only joking. I was only joking."

With eyes fixed on me as if I was hypnotisin' him, he takes the papermate out of the tray and moves away as if I might bite. (And I might.)

13

"What I want to know is who's in the team?" asks a gruff voice.

That's Stewart Pitt and he means the football team, of course. He's crazy about football and hopes to be the captain this year. He and I don't get along too well. Last year I had a fight with a brother of his called Ian, who's left now, good. Stewart's like his brother, bossy, with big ideas. I just don't ever want to get involved with his ideas. Most people think he's great. He's known as Stewpot and is a sort of hero to the little kids. I call him, Stewpid.

"I'm putting up a practice list tomorrow, and we'll pick the team from that," Sir replies, looking up from his desk. "And we shall be having a game this afternoon, just our year group, that is. Now, have you settled your places yet? I want to make a start on registers and dinner money."

I move to sit by Darren Parker, but Simon Singh gets there first and most of the other seats are taken by now.

"What's the matter? Not found a niche, yet?" asks Sir.

It's always the same. No place for me. Other people have friends. I have enemies. Not that I care. But there is one empty place. The face next to it smiles at me, nervously. I look away fast. No one wants to be smiled at by Heather.

"Hurry up," says Sir. "Just sit by Heather. She won't bite, you know."

Heather pats the chair and smiles again, a truly horrible sight. She must have forgotten a few things in the holidays, like the time I pushed her in the school goldfish pond. I lower myself into the chair, keeping as

14

far away as possible. Given a straight choice, I'd rather sit by a slug. Why on earth should I end up sitting by Heather? Bloomin' unfair. In a gloom at being at school in the first place and being next to Heather in the second, I push my hands into my jeans pocket—we aren't supposed to wear jeans at school—and discover some chewing gum, antique but welcome.

"Put that gum in the bin," says Sir, without looking up from the register. He must have eyes in the top of his head, under his hair. Life is going to be very tedious this year, I can see. I dump my gum in the bin, and sit down again, slumped, hands stuck in pockets. Exercise books, etc., are being given out. Heather shoots a look at me, then arranges mine for me with great care, as the usual dreary chat goes on about not wasting all the stuff, especially rubbers which are in short supply, apparently. So, under cover of the table I slice up the brand new white pure shining rubber with the one piece of equipment I did bring to school. My knife. (We're not allowed knives.) The rubber slices up neatly and prettily. And, I mean, what is a new rubber for if not to be spoilt? Like fresh snow, waiting for great big feet to trample on it.

Heather whispers spittily at me.

"You're supposed to put your name on your books."

"I know *that*. After all, I've been at this school for a million years."

I reach over and scrawl "Gowie Corby" in her purple felt tip. My books always end up looking like motorway disasters so I might as well begin as I mean to go on.

Heather is breathing heavily, like a sick cow.

"I'll do some for you," she utters, so I shove the lot in her direction.

She can get on with them if she wants to. Makes no difference to me.

"Suffering from paralysis, Corby?" asks Sir, looking up.

Heather turns a nasty shade of red, and pushes them back at me, so I scrawl my famous signature over the rest. Then Sir gives out the Maths books, and we do a rapid mental test to stir us up after the holidays, he says. I manage to make the rapid test very slow indeed, as I fail to understand any of the questions for some time, and before we've actually come face to face with any work at all, it's time to go into Miss Plum for what is down on the timetable as *Language*. Now, I know quite a lot of *Language*, some taught by my dad. But I doubt if Miss Plum would care for my sort of *Language*.

Miss Plum looks soft. Not like Mr. Merchant, Sir. I find a bit of chewing gum in another pocket.

She won't notice.

We move into the room. I manage to push over Jonathan Johns' tray, and stick a chair-leg in his back as he bends down to pick up all his bits and pieces. He swings back at me but I nip neatly out of range and grab a place at the back, near the radiator, a good place to be. Heather seems about to join me, no way, I say, and push out a seat for Darren instead, who's in one of his daydreaming moods, and doesn't know whether he's on this planet or on Jupiter. At last there is silence in that room, so I break it with:

"Are you a proper teacher, Miss?"

"Are you a proper boy?" she answers, quick as a

16

flash, no flies on this one even if she has long dark hair.

"I thought you might be a student. We get a lotta students here."

She doesn't answer me. "My name is Miss Plum," she addresses the rest of the class, and waits for a moment, but there isn't a flicker of a whisper or laugh, nudge, nudge.

" I hope we shall have a pleasant year together and do some interesting things," she goes on, and yes, miss, they all chorus like sheep bleating, baa, baa, the creeps. I jab the underside of the table with my little knife. She hands out cardboard.

"First, I should like you all to make folders to keep your work in, and record cards to record what you have been doing. You may decorate the folders if you wish, with a suitable picture or pattern, and remember to write your names clearly."

Soon we are all scribbling like crazy. I borrow Heather's new felt tips and draw bombs, machine guns and swastikas over mine, together with my sign, the vampire. It looks very nice and cosy when finished, so I sit and admire it, adding a few finishing touches from time to time. The teeth, with blood oozing, are particularly good. The buzzer goes for play and we surge back to our own classroom area, where Heather bears down on me like a female hippo with weight problems and offers me a pink biscuit.

"No, thanks, it's contaminated," I refuse it, and then she, suddenly, for no reason at all, shouts wildly at me, her chin wobbling, popping eyes glaring at me through her tatty hair, like an old English sheepdog with rabies.

"Why are you such a mean boy, Gowie Corby? What

17

makes you so mean? Why, you are the meanest boy in the class, the meanest boy in the school, the meanest boy in the world!"

This takes me by surprise, I don't know why she's getting at me, and so I mimic her wet, drippy, draggy, grotty, (spew-making) voice, except it's impossible to make it bad enough.

"And you, Heather Bates, are the stupidest girl in the class, the stupidest girl in the school, the stupidest female slob in the world."

She starts to cry, and the girls rush over to comfort her. Sir urges us outside to sample some fresh air, and I depart in search of chewing gum that I remember leaving stuck to the underneath of the washbasin in last year's cloakroom. There's just a chance that it might still be there if Buggsy, the caretaker, hasn't discovered it during the holiday.

The chewing gum has disappeared but several grotty little third-year kids are there, screeching like seagulls, when I go in, so I trip up one who looks like Heather, and I kick Graham Pitt, Stewpid's younger brother. He nearly gets me back but by then the cloakroom is in such an uproar that the teacher on duty, old Champers, puts his head—and his great big teeth—round the door to see what's going on, so I leave at speed, getting back into my classroom before the whistle blows for the end of play. Going back to my seat, I whip off one of JJ's pens in passing and, still passing, scrawl very rapidly all over Heather's folder, then drop the pen behind a cupboard, sit down and wait for them all to arrive and the wailing to begin. Heather is a terrible wailer.

"Sir, oh, Sir, oh, Sir, look what someone's done to the

folder I did for Miss Plum. Look! Look! It's ruined!"

Her eyes and nose are streaming, not a pretty sight. I watch with interest. I did a good job on the folder. No amount of rubbing out is going to restore that object to its former glory. It looks awful. I nod up and down in sympathy.

"What a mean thing to do," I say. "Never mind, Heather. Who did that mean thing to Heather's folder?" I enquire loudly of the class. No one answers me. Heather wails even louder if possible. Fancy actually caring about a folder. People are peculiar.

Sir looks angry. I nod up and down. JJ decides to open his gob. mouth

"It was probably Gowie Corby. It was probably Gowie Corby. He was always doing things like that, last year. It was probably Gowie Corby."

What a sneak. What a thing to say about me. Fancy picking on me like that when he couldn't possibly have known that it was me. I'm gonna get that sneaky so and so if it's the last thing I do.

"Don't listen to him. He's telling lies, Sir," I cry out.

"You're sure you didn't do it?" Sir asks me.

"No, of course not," I reply, feeling indignant, for JJ accuses me of everything.

"Does anyone else know anything about the folder?"

"That pen's an unusual colour," says Helen Lockey, a very bright girl. She has blonde hair, and is all clear and clean where Heather is muddy and blurry. "It's a greeny jade colour. There aren't many like that."

"Jonathan has one that colour," I say, helpfully. "He's got the biggest range, with all the colours."

"I didn't do it," he shrieks, hunting round like a mad

19

ferret. "In fact, my pen has gone. Gone. I can't find it anywhere. It isn't anywhere. He's got it. He's got it," he cries, pointing a shaky finger at me. I shrug my shoulders, hurt. I surely can't be the only villain in the class.

"You can search me," I offer. "I bet you won't find it on me." I feel fairly safe about this. Short of Buggsy shifting the cupboard, which is packed full of stuff, that jade-green pen can wait for a long, long time.

Sir sighs. "I should like to get on with the lesson, if you don't mind. Heather, you can make another one. And stop crying. Tears never repaired a ruined folder. I hope that no one does anything like that to anybody else's work ever again, while they're in my class. Or anyone else's," he adds.

Heather drops her work in the wastepaper basket, tears falling on it, like rain. At last the class settles to work, and Heather to sniffing. I don't feel like doing any more work. My timetable, maths, etc., are finished and the reading book I've been given looks about as interesting as cold stew. What I really enjoy is a horror story about vampires and the undead, werewolves and voodoo, witches and warlocks, ghosts and hauntings. I wish a vampire would get Heather. That would cheer up a dull morning if one flew in through the window, and settled quietly at Heather's throat, before Sir had noticed. But would a vampire want Heather? Not very likely, unless it was very starved of blood, hadn't had a tasty gorge for a long time. Moving off Heather, I think up a few tortures like Death of a Thousand Cuts, or the Iron Maiden, or the Water Torture, to try on JJ, but nothing seems really bad enough. I'll invent some of my own. Meantime, I flick one of the little bits of rubber in my pocket at Darren. It catches him neatly on the ear. Contact is made.

"Ow," he shouts. "I've been stung by a bee!"

Good ole Darren. He always gets things wrong. Except work, where he's always right.

"It was Gowie Corby," says JJ for the millionth time. He should have a recording made.

Sir looks really angry now. Will he blow up, I ask myself?

"Yes, it was Gowie," says Helen Lockey, and she is the sort of girl that teachers believe. "He flipped something at Darren. I saw him."

"Corby, come and sit here, away from the others, where you can't get into trouble. And work through this exercise for me."

"Yes, Sir," I grin, because I don't care. I'm used to sitting by myself as if I'd got rabies—a very interesting topic, rabies. I enjoy learning about rabies.

Anyway, anything is better than sitting by Heather.

In the afternoon the weather is really hot, the way it always is when you go back to school, after it's rained non-stop for the summer holidays. We play football and I score a goal, mainly because everyone except Stewpid is playing so badly that it's difficult to miss. At the end of the game Sir calls me over and says as if he was doing me a favour:

"Gowie, that wasn't bad. You've a fair turn of speed and you can head the ball, which is more than most of them can do. Come to the practice match with your kit, tomorrow lunch-hour."

21

"Haven't got any kit."

"What are you wearing now, then?"

"He took one of the third year's. I saw him. I saw him," puts in Jonathan Johns. Sir sighs heavily. He puts a hand on my shoulder. Tries to look into my eyes. No way. I don't like being conned into good behaviour.

"Look, you know you're not supposed to borrow other people's property without permission. You should have asked me for some. Haven't you brought your own kit to school?"

"No."

"Why not?"

"Haven't got any, Sir."

"Won't your mother buy you some?"

"You jokin', Sir?"

"All right. All right. I'll fix something for you. Only, don't take anyone else's again. Now, hurry up and get changed, the rest of you, and don't forget you've got a practice tomorrow."

He turns back to me. "Don't forget to replace that kit, Corby."

"I'll see he does. I'll see he does," says my friend Jonathan, but Sir has gone. I don't bother to reply to Creep No. 1, but as I change, a beam of sunshine, full of surprise at finding itself in our cloakroom, picks out something silver, the papermate in JJ's pocket, gleaming amid the immaculate school uniform. Using the fair turn of speed referred to by Sir, I slip in my vampire teeth, ever ready with the knife in my pocket, spike my hands into claws and give a fearful, deadly hiss.

"Jonathan Johns, the hour of your doom is

Gowie Corby Plays Chicken

GENE KEMP

FABER AND FABER
London · Boston

First published in 1979
by Faber and Faber Limited
3 Queen Square London WC1
Printed in Great Britain by
The Bowering Press Ltd
Plymouth and London

"Rosie's Prayer" was written by Rosie Bell
of St. Sidwell's Combined School, Exeter.

British Library Cataloguing in Publication Data

Kemp, Gene
  Gowie Corby plays chicken.
  I. *Title*
  823'.9'1J.   *PZ7.K3055*

  ISBN 0-571-11405-9

upon you, and you shall DIE . . . DIE . . . DIE . . .
AAARRRRHHHHHH!"

He leaps in the air as if ants have just bitten his bum,
and I reach out, grab the papermate, and shoot out
through the door, like I am breaking the sprint record.
Jonathan's still in his football boots, laces trailing, so I
have a head start as I rush across the playground to
where the crossing lady stands with her lollipop.

Behind me ring out beautiful howls of rage and
anger and fury. My heart sings. I find time to turn and
wave at him, purple, struggling.

"Come and get your pretty silver thing," I call out
to him.

"Give it back, you thief," he bawls after me, but I
spurt ahead, knocking over a coupla kids who start
bawling and bellyaching as well, but I don't stop to
investigate, because after all, I'm doing them a favour,
the sooner they learn that life is full of hard knocks the
better. Above the angry shouts of the mums I hear
another voice and take a quick shufti behind.

"I'll get him for you," Stewpid is shouting.

This means I shall have to hurry it up, for he can run
like a cheetah. I barge through the crowd of 'orrible
mums, snotty kids and prams that always litter up the
gate, and rush across the road, Mrs. Moggs, the crossing
lady, trying hard to keep up with me on her fat little
legs.

"Don't be in that much of a hurry," she pants.
"You've got all your life ahead of you. I think."

Down the street opposite, Spring Avenue, and towards the car park, where I head for a silver Ford
Granada, so that I can pause and hide a mo, to see how

23

the pursuit is going. And Simon Singh has joined in as well, which means I've got the two best sprinters in the school chasing me. But I can have a lot of fun before they catch up with me, if they ever do. Out of the car park into Reaper's Lane, fat lot of reaping is ever done there, and then round the corner and into the High Street, full of fat old housewives and layabouts, past Woolworth's and the Co-op and into Tesco's—perhaps I can lose them among the counters. I peer round a stack of Hovis loaves and see Stewpid just entering the doors with Simon right behind him, no Jonathan though, slow-footed halfwit. I mean to move on silently escaping, but I crash straight into a trolley, pushed by a bloke looking like one of the heavyweights in a James Bond film, so I leap away at speed as he snarls after me and knock over a pile of bean tins. Beanz meanz Bangs and Smashes, deafeningly loud, just missing two old geezers, who squawk and screech, and the whole store breaks out in—

"Kids, these days. . . ."

". . . ought to be locked up. . . ."

". . . discipline, that's what they need. . . ."

". . . no consideration for others. . . ."

". . . I blame the parents. . . ."

". . . ought to be stopped . . . punishment . . . bring back the birch. . . ."

"What's the world coming to?"

"Out of my way, you stupid old bags!" I yell, and run through the doors, going the wrong way, and the doorman calls after me, but I don't take any notice, it's old Charlie Baines, and he's a cripple anyway. I stay on the pavement for a minute only, then into Liptons,

24

hoping I can throw off the pursuers, straight through the shop to the multi-storey car park behind. I am starting to puff a bit now so I stop behind a Ford Capri and try to get my breath back.

And a cry goes up.

"Boy! You, there! What are you doing? You're not supposed to be here!"

I run on faster, stitch stabbing in my side, now. I feel like packing it in and going home. I'm out of the multi-storey now and still running, though slower. I hope the others have been copped by the attendants. This thought cheers me up, gives me fresh power, so I surge on again past Boots, towards the Library, ready to turn on to the New North Road that takes me back home. But I'm knackered now, shagged out, and looking back, see that Stewpid is gaining on me, has halved the distance between us, while Singh is coming up on my left. And I'm even more knackered, shagged out beyond thinking, legs moving in a dream, a dream of aching and longing to lie down and die. My breath comes in jags, my chest is going to explode. I keep running.

Help me now, Count Dracula.

The feet of Stewpid are right behind me now, pounding louder than my heart beats. Somehow I must get up the library steps, for if I can get in there before they reach me, they won't be able to duff me in. I don't want to be duffed in.

The sun is dazzling, shining through the leaves of the trees all around . . . it shines in my eyes, dazzling . . . burning me up. . . . A hand grasps my shoulder from behind.

"Got you, Corby!" gasps Stewpid.

25

"Oh, no, you ain't," I mutter, turning and twisting
and thrusting with my right boot.
Stewart falls clumsily down the steps.
And lands splat! on his right elbow.

Chapter 2

Mice, mice,
Are really nice,
Thumping about in their cage. . . .

Miss Plum says that they are both females, but I know she's wrong. She'll find out soon enough, and that should be funny. Nice little mice they are, one dark grey, the other butter-coloured. Miss decided we ought to have some animals in the classroom so she brought them for us.

"Let's choose their names," she suggests, as she gets us all back into seats again after the first inspection rush, not that anyone can see them as they've hidden themselves away in their upstairs room. It's a very good cage, with a wheel and proper drinking and food bowls, and branches for them to climb.

"I'll look after them, Miss Plum," I offer. So do about twenty other people.

"Have a rota," suggests Mr. Merchant, coming in at that moment. "And let me say, here and now, please note, Gowie Corby, that anyone who lets them out of that cage, without permission, is going to wish they had never been born. And, by the way, Gowie, are you coming to the hospital with me to visit Stewart, tonight?"

"What? Me?"

"Yes. You. After all, you put him there in the first place, thereby wrecking my football team by injuring its best player. Be ready for me when I call for you at six-thirty tonight. Take him something to cheer him up, fruit or something."

"I haven't got any money."

He sighs heavily. "All right. I'll fix you up with something."

I sink into a gloom, because I do not want to visit anyone in hospital, because hospitals are not the sort of places I like. Furthermore, I do not wish to see Stewart, and I do not think he will want to see me. Mr. Merchant apologises to Miss for interrupting her lesson, then goes out, after giving me a very dirty look.

Miss hands out bits of paper for name suggestions, and these she writes up on the board so that we can vote for them: Bubble and Squeak, Bill and Ben, Trish and Trash, Bangers and Mash, Fish and Chips, Starsky and Hutch and so on. I suggest Dracula and Frankenstein, but the names that get the most votes are Tom and Jerry.

"For crying out loud," says Darren. "You can't call them that. Tom's a cat, and he and Jerry are both males."

So we all vote again and get Tom and Jerry once more.

"The will of the majority," says Miss Plum, so we keep her talking for twenty minutes on what that means so that we shan't have to do any work. Lily

28

Wong makes a label for the cage with their names on, and after a time they come out and bang about a bit. Tom is the big fat grey one and the butter-coloured one is Jerry.

"Let's call their cage Mouse House," quavers Heather

"Freaky Fiends' Pad is much better," I say.

At playtime Heather pokes her finger through the bars and gets bitten by Tom.

"You'll probably get rabies from that," I tell her. "I know a lot about rabies. Shall I bring you some pictures I've got at home showing people in death agonies from being bitten by rabies?"

"Oooooh, ooooh, Mi—iss," she wails, sucking madly at the bitten finger. Miss pushes me outside as she tries to comfort the stupid cow. *girl*

I am sitting by the side of a hospital bed watching Stewart trying to open a box of chocolates that Sir has brought him from me, if you get it. Stewpid is up on traction, which means his arm is up in the air, so that he can't lie down at all, even to sleep. If he moves it at all—the elbow, that is—it won't set properly, and he'll be no good at football, ever. I haven't seen him since they took him away, screaming his head off, with Jonathan Johns telling everybody gathered round that it was all my fault, bloomin' unfair because I can't help it if Pitt has the kind of bones that break easily, can I?

Afterwards I have to go to the Headmaster and explain to him that running off with the papermate was all a joke and could I help it if people had no sense of humour?

"I'm glad you've got such a good keen one, then," he says to me, twitching his bushy eyebrows, "because you're going to need it to see you through writing letters of apology to Stewart and his mother for the anguish and distress you've caused them. And, Gowie Corby, just listen to me—" here I sigh as deadly boredom hits me, I've heard it all before—"I know you have problems, but so have other people, you know. You're one of mine—" here he smiles as if making a joke—"so do try to be more co-operative in school, adopt a more positive approach"—now what's he burbling about, I wonder?—"and stop being so awkward. We are only here to help you." And that's a laugh for a start, I think, looking at a horrible plant on the window-sill. It could have come straight out of a Dr. Who programme. Suppose it grew suddenly and swallowed him up and everyone was running round looking for the missing Headmaster. "Corby, are you listening to me?"

"Yes, Sir."

"Well, as I said before and shall now repeat again, you are not without ability"—now just what does that mean?—"and you could do well in your last year here, if you settle down and buckle down to it."

"To what, Sir? I don't follow you."

"TO WORK, OF COURSE. AND GAMES. WHAT DO YOU THINK I MEAN?"

"Yes, Sir."

"Oh, go away, Corby. And let me see those letters when you've finished them."

"Can I go now?"

"Yes, I said so, didn't I?"

"Yes, Sir."

30

"Oh, remember to come to me if you have problems or difficulties."

"I don't have problems or difficulties. I just have enemies."

With Mr. Merchant's assistance Stewart opens up the box of chocolates and offers me one with the hand that isn't attached to a pulley and the ceiling. I look round uneasily. For this place really gives me the creeps. I can't stand the smell. Really unhealthy. And all those nurses look like zombies, not that I mind zombies, proper spooky ones that is. I want to get out of here. Dangerous places, hospitals. You might be in here, harmless, visiting somebody, and before you could say Werewolves Unite they'd have you on the operating table, jacking both legs off.

I don't know what to say to Stewpid. I know I'm not saying sorry, because I said that in those letters I wrote, and then I had to copy them out again, because they weren't neat enough, and that's enough sorries for anyone.

"How are the practices going, Sir?" Stewpid asks.

"As well as can be expected without you there. I've made Simon Singh captain and we play Central next week."

"Is 'e in it?" he says, pointing the finger that's not on traction at me.

"Well, no. Gowie didn't turn up to any of the practices, did you?"

"You play on Saturday mornings, and I ain't givin' up my Saturdays for anyone."

"Why not, Gowie?"

"I've got better things to do."

"What better things?"

I shut my gob tight. Why can't he leave me alone? What I do on Saturday mornings is MY business, and he can poke his long conk in some place else. Get knotted, Sir. Let's change the subject.

"How do you go to the bog, all strung up as you are?" I ask the figure on the bed.

He goes a dirty red colour and wriggles about as much as he can considering his condition, and I wonder if he's shy, but then he explodes and I see that it's anger, not modesty.

"I use a bottle and a bed pan, thank you very much, thank you *very*, *very* much, Mister Bloomin' Corby, for getting me stuck in here when the football season's started!"

I shrug my shoulders, for no matter how mad he gets, he can't duff me in, he's stuck in bed, which is his hard cheese.

"You shouldn't have such rotten bones," I reply.

"Come along, you two," Sir says, sharp as a needle. "Let's have reasonable behaviour. Make an effort to get on with one another, at least."

"No way."

"Not likely."

"All right, all right. Calm down or you'll drive me insane. Now both say sorry."

Long silence.

"BOTH SAY SORRY."

We both say sorry. Huh.

Stewpid reaches for another choc, remembers me, and shoves the box towards me with his free hand. I manage to knock it on the floor, where the unwrapped chocs go on a neighbourhood tour. A nurse rushes forward tut-tut-tutting, and in the confusion, people bending over and so on, I somehow knock over Stewpid's orange juice, distributing it quite fairly over him, the nurse and the bed, to say nothing of the chocs, which I've never cared for much, anyway. Chewing gum's my favourite.

I look at my watch. Nearly time to go. I don't think Sir will bring me again, somehow. He'll leave me alone in the end. I know he's got his reputation as a good teacher to keep up, but that doesn't matter to me, I'm different, I'm not like this soft lot down here, my folks came from the North, descended from the Vikings, and I don't want to be liked, I don't want to be good, I don't want to be in the football team, or a useful member of anything, I don't want to know. I don't care.

Sir tries to talk to me on the way home, but I don't listen as I am thinking about the Peter Cushing film on later. I like the oldie horrors best, Boris Karloff and Bela Lugosi, but any horror is all right by me.

Back at school it's my turn to clean out the mice. You have to catch them and put them in a tupperware box while you do it. Some kids have already been bitten, because Tom is really wicked now and gets vicious when handled. I know why, because I know a lot about rodents, my best friends, the only ones I really care about, the ones I can trust. I've got some at home, and I can tell, when I pick Tom up, that she is pregnant. No one else realises this yet, and I'm keeping quiet. They're all so thick, except Darren, and he's only bright inside his head, he notices nothing going on around him. Tom twirls the wheel in fury after being handled, and I think about the baby mice, lovely little beasties.

You see, this school is open plan, which means there are no doors. Now, just imagine lots of escaping baby mice in an open plan school with no doors. What's more, the school is in a horrible mess because parts of it are being rebuilt and altered, right now.

When that bossy girl, Tyke Tiler, pulled half the school down just before the summer holidays, they decided that since they'd got to rebuild it in any case, they might as well alter it and make it modern at the same time. We thought we'd get a nice long holiday while they did this, but no way. We had to come back to school at the same time as usual, and get on with our lessons in all that noise and mess. Just how mean can people be? Very mean, if those people are anything to do with school. And so, here we are. Half the school roof's off, kids are being taught in the hall, in the canteen, walls are knocked down, new ones put up, cement mixers and earth-movers in the playground, pneumatic drills blowing, playgrounds out of bounds, sand and dust and piles of rotten wood and old furniture all over the place. We don't mind. The little mice don't mind. The teachers get a bit stroppy at times, though.

Like when, Miss Plum was reading this poem called "The Listeners". It's a bit wet, but spooky, and outside the room, a pneumatic drill buzzes away as she shouts out the words to us, when suddenly it stops and she is heard bellowing at the very top of her voice:

"And his horse in the silence champed the grasses...."

We fall about laughing while she does a cherry right up her neck and over her face.

Afterwards we are supposed to write out a poem for our folder; I don't, I do a fantastic picture of Heather being tortured in a deep dark dungeon instead, and my friends, the rats, laughing all over their little ratty faces. Miss says to put it in the bin, but I fold it carefully, and give it to Heather, with "For you Anything" written on it. And she is pleased.

Until she opens it.

Chapter 3

Hurry up, hurry up, step up the pace,
You silly old, silly old squashed tomato face.

I am singing to Heather who is walking just in front of me in the crocodile, "I'm walking behind you, you silly fat fool," and she keeps trying to escape by getting ahead, but each time I catch up, taking Darren, who is my partner, with me as I go. From time to time I tread on her and she wails a bit, but Sir is some yards away and does not see or hear.

It is Harvest Festival, and we are just going to the local church, and I give Heather just a little kick so that she can be a martyr. All the children are bringing gifts, except for Darren, who's forgotten as he forgets everything, and me, and that's because I just don't bring gifts for old people, it's encouraging them to go on living, which isn't right, they ought to be put down at fifty, they can't possibly enjoy life after that, can they? It would be much kinder to put them out of their misery, and then the rest of us wouldn't have to give 'em tins of beans and old packets of cereal and grub-eaten apples at Harvest Time. I wouldn't want that rotten ole rubbish, I bet they don't. They'd rather be dead.

We settle into church and while we sing "Come ye

Thankful People", the kids trail up to the altar with whatever they've got and put it on the altar steps. Now I am sitting next to Heather and for once I do not mind, for I see nestling in her lap, cosy, cosy, two cartons of eggs, and I uplift my voice with:

"There upon the golden floor,
Dropping bombs for ever more,"

which you've gotter admit is a lot more interesting than singing hymns.

And as I sing, I think what I am about to do.

Up the aisle trot the little ones, right little ghouls they are, and soon the steps are covered with all sorts of goodies, especially tins, and, even more, especially spaghetti tins. Lovely harvest. The fields of spaghetti must look really fantastic waving in the breeze. As I wait for them to get to our class, going last, I take a look behind me at the stained glass window, where the Saint is having her head chopped off by a peasant with a scythe. I quite like it.

It's our turn to go up. Heather has to push her way past Darren and me, as we aren't accompanying the rest, obviously. She gives me a nervous look, I can't think why, and I push out my knees to make it difficult for her so that she thinks she's getting left behind the others, and she starts flapping like a codfish, and about as pretty, and I nearly let her through, then I shove my right boot between her legs, and tangle her up so that she loses her balance. There's a song my mother sings when she's had a few, that goes "Something in the way she moves", well, that "She" isn't Heather, I never saw a worse mover as she arches her back, throws up her feet, lets out a screech and flings her eggs wildly in the air, finally collapsing in the aisle, while the eggs fly out of their cartons right over the boy now tripping over her and who just happens to be . . .

. . . and my voice rises up to the roof with joy. . . .
. . . Jonathan Johns. . . .

proudly carrying the biggest offering, he always brings the biggest, the great show-off, and it's a huge basket of fruit with cellophane and ribbon on it.

And JJ is showered with falling eggs, and Heather is wailing loudly from her seat on the floor. Miss Plum rushes forward and tries to clean up the egg juice off Jonathan with a very wee small handkerchief. Sir gets Heather to her feet and keeps the procession moving. The Vicar hasn't noticed, but then, he is deaf, and Darren hasn't noticed, but he is mad. I just hope that the Headmaster hasn't noticed, but I don't care, I'll worry about that later. Right now, we are about to sing :

"We plough the fields and scatter. . . ."

Singing loudly, I join in.

"The rotten eggs on the land. . . ."

And I turn round a little, full of happiness, so that I can see that interesting picture of the boring ole Saint having her head scythed off.

Happiness never lasts.

I tell Sir that it isn't my fault, that I can't help it if Heather has two left feet, no brain and a dozen eggs, but he takes no notice of what I say. Unfair. He tells me that I've got to help her with Maths for a week, and he'll test us both at the end of it. What a teacher. Any-

one else would give me lines or send me to the Headmaster. But this is worse, he knows I can't stand the
look or the pong of her, so it's MEAN. And if I'm not
kind and considerate to her, he says, he's personally
gonna wallop me with a plimsoll, one of his, since I still
haven't brought any.

Later. He wallops me with a plimsoll. Anything is
better than being kind and considerate to Heather.

Chapter 4

Ally ally onker
Mine's the best conker.

Conkers are everywhere at the moment, it's the season, and all the nutters are going for nuts. It's fairly boring, especially when JJ announces that he's the CHAMPION, showing off the most ginormous conker ever, polished and shining like his silly face. The playground is covered with string and bits of nuts.

Stewpid is back at school with his arm in plaster, and he *is* the big HERO with kids queueing to write their names on the plasterised arm. I say Hi to him and he hardly speaks back, which I consider mean. I don't care for that kind of meanness. After all, I haven't done anything to him. He began it all, chasing me. He isn't allowed to play football and has to go back to the hospital for treatment. The team is losing all its matches, Simon Singh is away with the flu and Pete Gillett, the goalie, is ill as well. So Sir has another go at getting me to play.

"I won't say that it's for the school, Gowie," he says, "for I know that interests you not at all."

" No, Sir."

"No, Sir? You mean no, it doesn't interest you, or no, you're not going to play?"

"Both, Sir."

"I thought I might get you to play for your own sake, because you enjoy the game."

"I don't."

"You look as if you do when you're playing."

"Load of rubbish. Sir," I add because he's looking a bit explosive.

"Just what do you enjoy? Apart from causing trouble?"

"Oh, Horror. I like that best. It makes me feel, oh, I don't know, cosy."

He twitches a bit.

"Go and sit down. No matter how I try, sometimes you depress me."

He looks so miserable that for once I don't kick Heather on the way back to my desk. But it's his own fault. Anyone who chooses to be a teacher deserves to have a rotten life.

At playtime Stewpid heaves over. He looks about as friendly as an anaconda with belly-ache from too much goat-swallowing.

"You listen to me, Corby," he says as if he was a hundred years old and me a little kid. "You gonna play for the team?"

JJ joins us, unasked.

"Don't ask him, Stew. He'll ruin it."

"It's already ruined at the moment. We're bottom of the league right now. The team needs you, Gowie, and the team comes first with me. Whatever you think, JJ."

His face shines with effort and love of the TEAM.

The TEAM comes above everything else. Even though he can't stand the sight of me, he'll do anything to get me to play if he thinks it will help, if he thinks it is the right thing to do. That's O.K. for him if he feels like that. I don't mind. He can get on with it. But he needn't expect me to. I don't give a bent penny for his pathetic TEAM.

"Don't bother, either of you. I wouldn't play for the team if they paid me. I've got better things to do."

And I walk off, leaving them standing there complaining. Considering JJ doesn't want me in it anyway, he's making an awful fuss about me saying no.

But Stewpid still follows me. He can't believe I really mean it.

"Look here," he begins.

"Where?" I ask, peering round.

"Oh, pack it in. This is serious."

"What's serious?"

"On Saturday we play Brent Hill. We've only got half a side and we need you, if we're to stand any chance for the Cup at all. Look, you've got to play."

"No, you look. Go and look for some of *your* friends, the Stewpot fan club, and ask them to play for your precious team. You're wasting your time with me. I don't want to know."

His face goes white, then red, and he raises his fist to me as if to hit me, thinks better of it, pushes his nose in the air and his voice down to his boots.

"You are the rottenest, meanest, horriblest kid who ever came here. You've never done nuthin' for nobody in the whole of your mean, miserable life!"

42

And I am suddenly angry. Why can't they leave me alone?

"Go and get knotted, Stewpid Bossy Boots Pitt. I ain't done nuthin' for nobody 'cos nobody's done nuthin' for me. Not ever. And they never will. And I tell you this. You've gotter look after yourself in this stinkin' world, 'cos nobody else will, and anyone who tells you any different is talkin' crap, that's what my Dad told me, before they put him inside. And that's what it's all about. See. Now leave me alone!"

And I am shouting my bloomin' head off to keep them all quiet, the Sirs and the Stewarts, I don't want 'em. No way. I push off into the bright sunshine, and across the playground. No one follows. The anger goes, no point in being mad, and I remember a tasty bit of gum I've got stashed in the classroom, and I fancy it.

By now, it's empty and there, just in front of me, shining like a polished mirror, is JJ's brief-case, brass bits glowing like gold. I open it. Spotless books nestle in a spotless lining, pens, etc., in a separate partition. I look at what he's reading. Yuck.

"That's Jonathan's," squarks Heather, putting in an unlovely appearance from nowhere.

I reach for super glue on the shelf, the extra strong kind that sticks wood and so on. I pull off the top—it's almost full, lots of gooey, gorgeous glue. I tilt it over the case.

"You mustn't do that," blethers Heather, like an old sheep. Typecasting.

At the bottom of the case is Super Conk, the Champion. I pick it out with loving care.

"Wanna bet?" I ask, stamping on the conker with

43

maximum power as I empty, glug, glug, glug, the glue into JJ's pride and joy, and the slurping noise is music, music, music to my ears. The glue covers the books, the pens, everything, and I spread it generously around the fastening before I close it up. For ever, maybe? The conker lies shattered in bits on the floor, string still attached. I turn to Heather, who's all eyes and gob. *mouth.*

"If you tell anyone who did it, I shall come to your house at night, when you're in bed, and I shall climb into your bedroom and strangle you. After I've finished torturing you. And you'll be dead for ever."

I feel her eyes watching me and I hear a little sob as I whistle into the bright morning, feeling at one with the world.

Sir's questions go on and on, but we miss a lot of work, which suits me fine. JJ keeps saying my name over and over again. As I point out to Sir, it's unfair the way he automatically accuses me of everything. Heather sits like a stuffed sheep, keeping quiet, quiet.

Only the mice are really cheery, bumping round on their wheel, which squeaks 'cos it needs oiling. No one has a clue that Tom is pregnant. Stewpot is in a filthy mood and the team's morale is really low. And on Friday when I breeze in, fairly cheery, 'cos it's nearly Saturday, I find a note waiting for me. It says:

"LOOK OUT CORBY YOUR GOING TOO GET WOTS COMING TO YOU."

Then when we come out of Assembly there's another. "DEATH TO YOU SCUM."

I don't find that nice at all, and spend most of the morning watching them all, wondering who sent it. The last one of the day reads:

44

"WE'VE GOT A GANG ONTO YOU ROTTEN SWINE AND WERE GOING TO DUFF YOU UP SO YOU WISH YOUD NEVER BEEN BORN, SO LOOK OUT YOU BEAST."

Pathetic.

Some time later, near hometime, I don't find it so pathetic. At the end of a long, draggy, boring Friday afternoon, it's at last time to clear up. Soon, very soon, the classroom empties, only Heather and a coupla girls left, and Darren, who's reading and has forgotten he's supposed to be going home.

"Where is everybody? They disappeared fast," I say.

The girls' faces go tight and closed up. I know that look. It means that someone is being kept out of the know, and it's often been me in the past, and it's me now.

"Somethin's goin' on," I say to them.

The girls move away, but I stop Heather near the door, seize her right ear and twist it. She squeals. The other two depart as if there are bombs in the classroom.

"Now talk. What's goin' on?"

"Nuthin'." She whimpers as I twist a little harder and drag her to the cloakroom, to keep out of Merchant's way.

"Talk."

"They're gonna duff you in."

"Where?"

"Outside school. . . ."

"Who?"

"They'll hurt me if I tell you. . . ."

"I'll hurt you worse. You're just born unlucky. Talk."

"Ow. Please. Don't."

"I'll stop if you tell me who's in it."

"The team, mostly."

"Why?"

"They're fed up with you 'cos you're so horrible. Oh, stop, stop. I'll tell Sir."

"No, you won't."

"Let me go. Please, oh, please."

"Where are they now?"

"You usually go to the shop on the corner after school, for some chewing gum."

"Who told you?"

"Everybody knows."

"Go on. . . ."

"They're waiting for you in the alley way at the back of the shop. That's all I know, honest. Let me go, now."

"Get out." I push her through the door. She makes me feel sick. I feel sick anyway. Some of the kids in the team are a horrible size. Stewpid is bigger than Mr. Merchant. Not that he'll be doin' much with *his* elbow.

I walk slowly into the playground. Most of the kids have gone home by now. What am I to do? Fancy that lot ganging up on me. I must go very carefully. Think . . . think. I'd better go another way home, the long way round.

And Miss Plum walks through the playground carrying two heavy bags, and in a flash I am beside her, smiling a face full of teeth like Tom in a Tom and Jerry cartoon.

"Miss Plum, please let me carry your bags. You look so laden."

She looks surprised as well. My nice smile is almost

46

splitting my face. She hands over the bags and we walk along side by side. I start to talk to her.

"I expect that you are looking forward to the week-end, Miss Plum. It must be a relief to get away from an awful mob like us."

"Oh, you're not that bad, really. But you are right in a way. I do enjoy the weekends."

"Have you a hobby, Miss? I like to go bird watching when I get the time."

"Do you indeed, Gowie? Now, that's very interesting."

On we walk, discussing hobbies, like two old geezers, and she tells me how nice it is to talk to me like this, as sometimes she feels she hasn't got to know me as well as she would have liked. The corner shop comes into view, with JJ's ugly mug peering round it, and jerking back at the sight of me, and I am killing myself with laughter inside as Miss Plum and I walk right past, together. I bet they're mad. I bet they're astonished. I smile at Miss Plum with all my available teeth. She does a cherry. We go right past and down the road and I'm safe. I've mucked up their dirty little plan. Load of morons. On we go, well away from the scene of danger.

"I catch a bus here," she says. "Thank you for your company, Gowie."

She smiles at me as if she really likes me. I could fancy her if she wasn't so old and a teacher.

"'Ave a good weekend, Miss."

I run on till I come to the cul-de-sac where I live, Nelson Place, for heroes to live in, my grandad used to say. There are only three terrace houses, and a ware-house and some trees opposite. My house is the last one. The house next door has been empty for ages, ever since old man Pearson went bananas in the middle of the night, and chased his old woman outside in her nightgown. Round and round a car they ran in the moonlight with him waving a knife at her. I was watching out of the bedroom window and in the end the police arrived and took old Pearson away, then she left and since then the house has been empty.

I run along, happy with the Friday freedom feel, all the weekend stretching ahead, just for me, nobody saying do this, do that, go here, go there, Gowie Corby. And it's even better because I've outwitted the TEAM, and there should be something good on telly tonight, and I wonder what there is to eat. I get out my key and open the door, and suddenly, crash, stab, bam, bang, I am hit from behind, all hell breaks loose, and pain swells from nowhere to everywhere till I want to scream, and I go down on my knees, I'm jumped, ambushed, boys everywhere, hitting, kicking, I try to cover my head, my body. The pavement's hard, it tears my trousers, gashes my knees, scrunch, scrape, blood, warm and wet. Blood and salt in my mouth, tears pouring, singing in my ears, I can't see, I'm hurt, I'm scared, I can't think, I can't fight, there are too many of them, help me, help me somebody, help me please, why won't somebody come, help, no one will, no one ever did, no one, there's only you and all of them . . . lie still . . . play dead . . . lie still . . . lie dead . . . perhaps I am dead . . . voices above the grunts. . . .

"That's for Stewart's elbow . . ." I feel sick.

"Are you sorry, Corby?" Oh, stop, leave me.

"Say you're sorry, Corby." I feel sick. Leave me alone . . . alone. . . .

48

Stewart's voice. Gruff. Anxious? Far away?

"Pack it in. We've gone too far . . . come on. . . ."

It's dark. I hurt. Help, help me. . . .

Another noise, a different voice. A door opening? A voice like those on the telly, cutting through the noise.

"What are you doing? Are you mad? Leave him alone!"

And everywhere is filled with the sound of running feet, running away. Someone drops down beside me, hands lifting me, and tears fall on me, mixing with mine.

"How could they do this to you?" cries the voice like those on telly.

And that's how I first meet Rosie Lee.

Chapter 5

Moonlight, starlight,
The bogey man's not out tonight.

"That's a funny name for you, a girl like you," I mutter through the swelling of my face. She is cleaning me up with huge clouds of cotton wool, softer than soft, like a mother cat cleaning her kittens, and she looks at me closely the way I look at the little mice, and I ought to mind, but I don't. I have no pride. I just sit, a disaster area, on the sofa, in front of the fire where she half dragged, half carried me. From time to time she makes tutting and clucking noises, all in this American telly accent, yes, even her tuts have this different sound, which was the first thing I ever noticed about her, centuries ago outside on the pavement. All her sounds come out different shapes. Feeling around with some care the one enormous bruise that is me I don't think I am much damaged, only the face growing like a turnip from where it came into contact with the pavement. But I don't mind sitting here, warm, relaxed, being fussed over. The folks I've known aren't noted for fussing, especially my Mum.

"Everyone says that," grins Rosie, and I stare in fascination at her teeth, more teeth than I've ever seen in one face, and covered with a brace the size of the Forth Bridge. "What's your name?"

I remember my teeth and fish for them in my pocket, they're safe and I wave them in front of me, for I can't bear to stick them into my puffy gob, and she giggles, I hate girls who giggle, but not this one, and I start as well, but it hurts too much so I stop very quickly.

"Count Dracula."

"Kinky, eh? Oh, I like you, Count Dracula."

She pours some evil-smelling liquid on to the cotton wool and before you can say The Curse of Frankenstein she is putting it on my eye.

"What's that?" I shriek. "Poison?"

"No, witch hazel."

"I told you, it's witches' brew. Evil."

"No, magic. Now, sit still, while I fix something for you to drink, and you'll feel so much better."

She stands up and she's taller than me, a big girl.

"Hey, how old are you?"

"Twelve. I was twelve last August. I'm a Leo."

"Oh, you're older than me, then. Mine's on Christmas Eve." I'm always proud of that. Different. "Capricorn."

"They're grabbers."

"Leos are bossy. Especially Leo girls."

"I know. Now don't move and I'll be back."

I am so tired I sort of doze off in the warmth of the fire, and then she is back, with a tray, and there's a pink drink with ice cream on the top and chocolate shreds, and soup, and a slice of something, what's that? I ask.

"Pizza," she says. "Eat it, my momma's pizza is better than anybody's."

I'm not arguing, though I have to eat slowly. I am feeling a bit muzzy, like when Mum lets me join her on the gin, and everything seems strange.

"You're not real," I say slowly. It seems to take a long time to say, but then it doesn't matter, nothin' matters.

"What do you mean when you say, I'm not real?" she asks, taking over the soup and spooning it to me as if I am a two-week-old baby, no, not two-week, too weak, I smile feebly inside at that.

"Where did you come from? And all this food? You're a . . . ghoul . . . that's what you are, and you'll get me in your power, but I shall prevent you."

"I am not a ghoul," she shouts.

"You're a fig . . . of my imag . . . imagination."

"I'm not a fig, nor a ghoul, and I think you mean to say figment. But I am a person, a girl, Rosie Angela Lee, aged twelve, late of Pittsburgh, Pennsylvania, U.S.A., and now living next door to you in number 2 Nelson Place. We moved in earlier today, and I was just sorting things out when I heard you and those monsters, and I came out to help. Gee, I didn't know kids could be like that. Thugs. Near murderers."

Her eyes shine bright with anger, and I think I wouldn't want to quarrel with Rosie Angela Lee. I close my nearly-closed eyes.

"Hey," she says. "I'm gonna leave you now to have a rest. I'll come back later and see that you're all right. Don't worry, now. You'll be all right on your own. I'm not far away."

I nearly manage to tell her that being on my own is nothing to me, I've been on my own more often than I remember, but it's too much trouble, I'm too tired. I do not hear her go.

It's dark when I wake up, with only the glow of the gas fire to light the room. First, I do not know where I am, and next I ache, oh, how I ache, and with the ache I remember it all, the fight on the doorstep, no, not a fight, a disaster for me, yet not a disaster because of the girl, Rosie, I must've dreamt her, with her smile and brace and teeth, and her gold-rimmed spectacles catching the light, and her giggles, and a door opens, there's a soft noise beside me, and:

"Are you awake?"

I manage a low, vampire noise, pretty good, considering it's not easy with a swollen mush. There is a giggle for an answer.

"Good, you're awake, Count Dracula. I'll put on the light, so you can emerge from your coffin."

"In the family vault. You can be Ghoul No. 1, Rosie."

"I'm not at all sure that I want to be a ghoul, though you keep making me into one. What is a ghoul, anyway?"

"It's a spirit that eats corpses. Nice. Nothing like a juicy bit of corpse, Rosie."

"I can probably acquire a taste for it in time, like eating greens," she answers, switching on the light. "Gee, your house is so nice and peaceful. . . ."

"Like a tomb."

"Sure, if you say so. I just meant in comparison with ours. Belinda is fighting Amy. They are not nice little girls at all, especially Belinda, and Poppa has just smacked Joe, who is kinda nice, but not at all disciplined, and it's a whole loada trouble in there."

"Is that your family?"

"Sure. And that reminds me. I have to ask you, if your mother and father and you, of course, would care to come and take coffee or a drink with us, later this evening. And anyone else in your family, of course. After all, since we're gonna be neighbours, we may as well get to know each other."

I get up to look with interest at my mush in the mirror, examining all the lumps and bruises as best I can through the eye that is still open. Just. Not a pretty sight, Count Dracula, I say to it, and then to Rosie:

"My mother works at a club every night, and on Friday there's an extension so she doesn't get home till after midnight."

"Will your father come along?"

"My Dad walked out on us. Some time ago."

"Oh." I watch her face in the mirror. She turns away. I cannot see her face and specs.

"And you're an only child?"

"I've got a brother. Mark."

"Can he come along?"

"No, he's away as well. He's at reform school for pinching ciggies from a kiosk. He's pinched things before, but this time they got him."

"Oh, Count Dracula. . . ."

"He only did what the rest did, but he didn't run fast enough. He was always a bit slow on his pins, our Mark. That's the real crime, getting caught, Rosie." I try to see her face so that I know what she's thinking. I want to see her face a lot. But I go on, I don't have to tell her but I can't stop.

"My Dad's in the nick. . . ."

"What?"

"Prison. Gaol. For stealing, though he'd left us before that anyway. You know, I don't miss Mark, but I miss my Dad. He used to tell me jokes and play football and give me pocket money. My Mum forgets, she does."

Rosie sits down on the chair and pulls at the cotton wool lying on the arm.

"My brother Joe was the best of us. He was smashin'."

"Was?"

"Joe's dead. He bought it last year, oh, I can't remember when."

"Bought it? Bought what?"

"Got killed, Rosie. He was mad on motor bikes. And he got killed on one. And that's why there's only me here, any more."

She gets up and comes to the mirror and looks at it with me, and our faces look back at us, and mine is all lumpy, and hers doesn't match in the mirror, each side looks different, and tears are pouring down her cheeks, and:

"Oh, Count Dracula," she sobs, and at that moment a smell of burning comes up very strongly indeed, and looking down, I see that my trousers, already torn, are scorching, and they start to burn my legs and owch, I yell, jumping backwards, very nippily, and we start to laugh, and soon we are shouting with laughter and rolling about the floor. At last we sit up, and she wipes her eyes, and—

"Ooh, I do hurt," I complain.

"You'd better throw those trousers away, they've had it," and "Oh, poor Count Dracula, no family," says Rosie.

"Whadya mean? First of all, I'm not poor, I'm great, and get this straight, Ghoul No. 1, I hate people, most people, that is, I like being a loner. And I do have a family."

"You do? Not that it matters, you have me, now."

"You're soppy, Ghoul."

"No, I'm not."

"Yes, you are. Now you come and meet my folks. They're not soppy. And promise me, on the Vault of Frankenstein. . . ."

"I promise."

"You don't know what it is, yet. . . ."

"I guess you're gonna make me promise not to tell anyone about what you're gonna show me."

"You're so sharp you'll cut yourself if you're not careful. Yes, you're right. Say after me, I promise on the Vault of Frankenstein never to tell anyone what I show you now."

"I promise."

My family, my friends live in our cellar, which I've got to myself now that Mark isn't here any more. We used to share it. It's big, filling all the length of the house, with two tiny windows at each end, and a dim light under the stairs for when you go down the steps. The cellar is dark even in the daytime.

"See how I fixed it up," I whisper to Rosie. It's a whispering sort of place, and she is very quiet, only her

56

eyes a-gleam behind her specs. If she had talked her head off I was going to push her out and bolt the door against her, even if she did save me in the doorway attack.

I've put two old tables underneath the little window that looks up to the back yard, and there's shelving fixed along the sides and here I keep the cages where my family live.

First the gerbils, Zombie and Voodoo. They have had babies, but I sold them to the pet shop. Zombie, the female, is bigger than Voodoo and she bullies him, she's De Big Boss. When she hears me she rushes forward for her nut, a shelled monkey nut, then charges upstairs with it to add it to her collection, and comes downstairs again, making chirrupy noises so I'll give her another, which I do. Voodoo waits in the background till she lets him have one. He's a creepy sorta gerbil.

Next the mice, who vary in number a lot, depending who's had babies. Right now, there's a fat brown and white bachelor called Terror, only he's not, he's slow and lazy, and then two white red-eyed females, Ghoulie and Weird, and a family cage—a dark-brown male, Lurch, with his little grey mate, Witchie, and they have a family of seven, very small in a heap of paper in the corner.

Zombie is whiffling and scrabbling and kicking her back paws, so I take her out and give her to Rosie, who lifts her to her face, and she scrabbles in her hair and sniffs her ears. And last of all, I come to my favourite, Boris Karloff, my black and white rat. He is brilliant. He's clever and smart and he loves me. He is waiting for me to come, because I am late, with falling asleep

57

and everything. I get him out of his cage and he runs over me, and I love the feel of his fur and his feet running over me. His face is sharp, his eyes are bright and his tail is long. Soon, I'm gonna get him a mate, and then we'll have lots of little ratty persons.

My mother doesn't know about Boris, in fact, Rosie is the only person who does. She knows—my mother does —that I've got mice down here, but she doesn't mind, she says, so long as I keep them out of her way and keep them cleaned out properly, and I do.

We go back upstairs, at last, with Zombie and Boris, and watch telly till Rosie goes home. I put Zombie back but I keep Boris with me as I sit up to wait till Mum comes in. He's good company, his sharp-clawed little feet running over me. He sniffs at the witch hazel and we settle quietly together.

Chapter 6

Hick, hack, hoe
My first go.
I'll split you yet
And you'll forget
That it's your go.

I dribble my tennis ball through the playground, hands in pockets, wearing my biggest boots, and everyone looks. Everyone stares. For my eye is turning nicely all the colours of the rainbow and my face looks like a ploughed field.

"Ugh," says one little ghoul from the first school. "Are you goin' rotten, then?" I pull a really horrible face at her and she runs away screaming. Not a bad start to Monday morning. I stroll into the classroom and who should be waiting there but Heather checking the innards of a polythene bag, so I creep close and shriek right down her lug-hole.

"Ooh-erh!" she screeches just like a steam engine letting off steam, and I push my face near to her with my vampire teeth in; my face doesn't hurt any more although it looks so bad. Still screeching, she drops a packet of sandwiches which I quickly manage to tread on.

"Oh, Heather, I am so sorry. However did I manage to do that? Let me help you pick them up."

So I bend down, joining Heather who is in full grovel, like a berserk hippo that has lost its young, and I scatter the rest of the sandwiches. Heather is wailing loudly by now, and the girls are rushing up, clucking, talking about fetching Sir. In the meantime I look up to see JJ smirking at my face, so I raise my right boot to him and he stops smirking.

And Sir comes in. With a big girl behind him. It's Rosie. I didn't know if she'd be in this class or the other one. She's chewing her bottom lip, a bit nervous, looks for me and gives a half grin. All the kids stare at her, my face forgotten.

"Get into your seats, everyone," he says. "Heather, what is the matter? Oh, I see, you've dropped your sandwiches."

"It was Gowie Corby. Gowie Corby did it," says JJ.

"And I haven't got any dinner, now," wails Heather.

"Quiet, everyone. Heather, put those unlovely fragments in the bin and stop mourning over them. I'll deal with the problem of your dinner in a moment. Now I want you all to meet Rosie Lee, who's going to be here with us, for a time, anyway. Rosie is from the States and I want you to make her especially welcome, show her the ropes and generally look after her. They're not a bad crowd, Rosie, they could be worse, though not much. Choose yourself a seat."

The girls all move invitingly, being eaten up with curiosity, I suppose.

"Come here. By me. Rosie," go the whispers, and above them all booms Stewpid's voice.

60

"Strewth. It's her."

"Who?" asks JJ.

"The girl," says Simon Singh.

"What girl? What girl?"

"The girl in the doorway, of course," Simon hisses.

I hear all this as I examine under my table thoroughly for lurking chewing gum. If Rosie wants to sit by the girls, she can. If she doesn't want to know me that's O.K. by me.

"She's a funny-looking bird," says JJ.

"I'll sit here," smiles Rosie, pulling up the empty chair beside me at my rabies table just under Sir's conk. And she turns the full stretch of her brace on me.

"Equip her with a tray, paper, pencils, etc., please, Gowie."

"Yes, Sir."

He's spotted my face. He blinks and looks again.

"Good lord. Have you been taking part in *Dr. Who*?"

"Somethin' like that, Sir."

"Er—come and see me in a little while, mmh?"

I collect up bits and pieces for Rosie. "Yes, Sir."

"What about my dinner?" wails Heather, after all, she hasn't been heard, lately. The class is on edge, looking at Rosie or me, or watching Sir, and in the middle of it all, Heather wails again.

"I shan't have any dinner to eat."

Stewpid can't take his eyes off Rosie.

The girls are whispering again.

"What's he done?"

"It looks horrible." (I agree.)

"He's a battered baby." (Tee hee, horrible bunch.)

"I know what happened. I'll tell you. Later."

"Mary Spray saw it *all*. She was watching. . . ."

"Look. Gowie's being *nice* to that new girl."

"What's come over him?"

"I know *why*."

"Tell me. . . ."

"Not *now*."

"Gowie Corby wrecked Heather's packed lunch, Sir."

Sir marks the register and then the dinner sheet. And at the end he looks up and silence falls, the whispering stops. He sends Lily Wong and Tracy, her friend, to the office with the register and we wait in total silence till they come back. And still he does not speak. At last he starts to talk, quietly and fast.

"Heather, what happened to your lunch?"

"Gowie Corby made her drop it." JJ again.

"I want Heather to tell me. Did Gowie knock it out of your hand?"

"No."

"What did he do then?"

"He shouted down my ear and I dropped it."

I can't swear to it but it seems as if a smile appears for a minute on his face.

"And that's just what we're going to do now, Heather dear, we're going to drop the whole subject. I shall treat you to a cooked school dinner."

"But I don't like school dinner."

He roars suddenly: *"Then you'll have to lump it the same as I do*!"

And in the same breath,

"Jonathan Johns!"

Jonathan jumps in the air like a frog that's just discovered he's world champion.

62

"Little boys of five tell tales, Jonathan. Boys of twelve do not. Now, if I hear you mention Gowie Corby's name again this term, then you're out of the team as we do not have babies in it."

JJ sits dumbstruck, face yellowish-green.

"Finally, since I specially dislike whispering of the kind that's going on at the moment, perhaps Gowie will tell us all what's happened to his face and then we may be able to get on with—you may have heard of it— WORK."

Then he smiles straight at me.

"But if you don't want to say anything, Gowie, just keep them guessing."

Everyone watches and waits, watches and waits. You can feel the quiet.

And I sit still, eyes wandering round the room, picking them out, Stewpid, JJ, Pete Gillott, Raymond Davies, Simon Singh, Tim Adams (but not Darren, reading *Black Holes in Space*, not knowing what's going on). Just the TEAM, from this class and next door. (I hope Sir doesn't think I'm battered, Mum's not the battering type, though Dad had his moments.)

I'll tell him who did it. I'll tell him who the rotten, mean, bullying cowards are. Call themselves a TEAM, what a lousy stinking bunch. British sportsmanship at its best. I don't mind sneaking, telling tales about what they did. I don't mind telling Sir at all, letting him know that his precious TEAM are gang-bangers. Thank you, Sir, for this TEAM. Thank you, TEAM.

They are looking everywhere but at me, and Stewpid has turned bright scarlet. He looks as if he might cry. Simon Singh is looking down his long nose, as if he wasn't in the classroom at all. The girls are waiting, like cats waiting for cream. . . .

"Sir, it was . . ." I begin. Only Rosie smiles at me.

". . . playing on a swing in the park, Ifelloffandmyfacedraggedalongthegroundanditwasn't . . . anybody's . . . fault . . . Sir."

And the smile on Rosie's face widens till it's the biggest thing on earth, and she hasn't got hundreds of teeth, she's got thousands! I gotta grin back and soon the whole class is grinning and Sir says:

"Let's get on with some work then, for Heaven's sake and mine as well. A mental test, I think. Going to try for a change, today, Gowie?"

"Yeah, I mean, yes, Sir."

And I go at speed, finishing first—except for Darren of course, we don't count him, he doesn't mind—but Rosie comes galloping in second.

Huh, it's gonna be tirin' if I take to this workin' stuff.

Chapter 7

Eeny meeny mink monk
Chink chonk chow
Oozy boozy vacadooz
Way vie vo—vanish

We make our way into the playground, that is full of machines and dust.

"Don't go round that side of the school," says the teacher on duty who happens to be Miss Plum, drinking her coffee, hands round the cup for warmth and comfort, I think, for she looks dead miserable, as she sends kids away from the sand and cement mixers and dust and noise and old timber that's being pulled out of the building like rotten teeth out of somebody's head, with pneumatic drills roaring like a dentist in hell.

"I've never seen a school like this before," says Rosie in a shout.

"It's not always been like this. It's the new building going on."

"What for?" she yells.

"A girl called Tyke Tiler. . . ."

"What? I can't hear you. . . ."

We move away a bit. So does Miss Plum.

"This girl, Tyke Tiler, pulled down the clock tower,

and they had to rebuild that anyway, so they decided to alter it at the same time and make it all up to date."

"You see what I mean. Having a clock tower pulled down by a student is not the normal kind of happening to occur."

"I wouldn't know."

"What are you laughing at?"

"Your funny English."

"It's you English that are funny, crazy. I have attended a great many schools, because of my father travelling about a lot, and I think this looks the craziest yet. Interesting, though."

"You two, come away from there. All this dust is no good for you. To say nothing of the noise," says Miss Plum as a particularly loud blast sounds off behind us. She smiles at Rosie, who says,

"Do you like teaching with all this going on around you?"

"No, I didn't think it would be at all like this. But it won't last for ever. Eventually the building will be finished and all will be quiet and peaceful. You're the new girl, aren't you? What's your name?"

Rosie tells her, then says,

"And now you tell me that's a funny name for me to have."

"I shan't be as rude as that, probably because I've suffered with mine," and she lowers her voice. "Some children call me Little Plum," and as Rosie looks bewildered, "That's out of a comic called *The Beano*," she explains, "and—GOWIE CORBY, WHAT HAVE YOU DONE TO YOUR FACE?"

66

"Didn't you notice, Miss?"

"No, how could have I missed it?"

"I fell off a swing in the park, and my face got dragged along the ground," I say, quite easily now, in fact if I say it much more often, I shall start to believe it myself.

"Well, take great care of it. You must have had a lot of pain," says Little Plum, peering with great sympathy at my disaster area.

"She is real nice," says Rosie with fervour as we round a corner, to where the front door had stood once, it's very hard to imagine now, and there, dark and cavernous, a great gaping hole lies in front of us.

"Oh, Frankenstein!" I cry, as the whistle goes for the end of play.

Back in the classroom, everyone is talking about the cellar, which is what the hole is, an ancient cellar underneath the school, and opened up by the workmen when they started to knock down the Headmaster's old room and the office. It's very old indeed, they say, older than the school itself, probably centuries old, dating back to really ancient buildings that have stood before on that spot, because our school is one of the oldest in the country, and the church we go to was first built by the Saxons in seven hundred and something.

Skeletons, breathes somebody, there are skeletons down there.

"Who says there are?"

"Buggsy's seen them with his own eyes."

"Well, he wouldn't see them with somebody else's,

would he?" says Darren, actually drawn out of his reading about space, and taking notice of what's going on here on this planet, for a change.

"Could be Roman skeletons."

"Or Viking. Or skeletons from the cholera epidemic that Sir told us about when nearly half the children in the school died!"

A wail hits the air. "I want to go home, if there's skeletons."

"Don't let me stop you," I say to Heather, as I open the door for her to go. "Yes, the cholera germs do stay with the skeletons and you can catch it easily. And cholera is nearly as bad as rabies. You die in horrible pain."

She is wailing really well as Sir comes in, looking excited.

"Shut up, Heather," he says, and she is so surprised she stops quite still with her mouth wide open.

"Tell us all about it," we say.

"About what?" he grins.

"Skeletons in the cellar."

"What cellar? What skeletons?" But he is still grinning.

"Don't be mean. You know all about it, Sir, because you wrote that book on the history of the school."

"Yes, but I didn't know anything about the cellar then. I didn't know it existed."

"Have you been down there yet, Sir?"

"Yes, I've been down with Mr. Buggit. They're closing it up again quite soon, because they don't think it's safe to leave it open with all the children about."

"Shame. What's it like? Is it haunted?"

"Quiet now. Yes, there are the remains of a few skeletons down there. . . ."

"Oh, oh, oh. . . ."

"Heather, a few old bones won't hurt you. . . ."

Some of the other girls were twitching a bit by now, as well as Heather.

"I knew this school was different," whispers Rosie. "I expect you've been busy in that cellar, Count Dracula."

"How did you guess?" I whisper back.

"Ve 'ave de vays ov finding out," she hisses at me.

"Can you take us down there? Please?"

"I don't want to go. Not with skeletons!"

"Tell us what it's like down there."

"It's older than the school, which is mid-Victorian, and I think it probably dates from late Mediaeval times, like a lot of this city. In one corner there's an interesting arch, which could be even earlier, possibly Norman, and it was in this corner that the workmen discovered the skeletons, three of them actually, buried under a pile of rubble. I am hoping for a few more interesting remains, pots or tools perhaps, we shall have to wait and see. Otherwise, the cellar itself is very dusty and cobwebby, there are some shelves, a few old desks, and an empty cupboard, all Victorian."

"Were you scared when you saw the skeletons?"

"Well, no. I didn't do them any harm and I don't suppose they'll do any to me. You're not scared of the bones your dog chews, are you? Well, I'm not scared of three old skeletons in the school cellar and I hope that you wouldn't be, either."

"Who do you think they were?"

"I imagine they were cholera victims, from the epidemic in the eighteen-thirties, probably, when this school, in an earlier building than this, remember, was turned into a hospital, and a great many people died here. Later on the cellar was boarded up for some reason, and then forgotten in time."

"What are they going to do with them?"

"Well, they have to be examined by the official authorities, which always has to happen, no matter how old the bones in question may be. Then they'll probably be buried in peace, the cellar closed up once more, and all trace of today's discovery forgotten."

He sounds as if he is sorry.

"I wish they'd keep it open."

"Yes, it does seem a pity in a way, Gowie, but the authority have decided that it would be a risk to the school generally, and we must abide by that."

"Is it haunted, Sir?"

"What, our school? Never."

A low moaning noise is heard from Heather, and this makes Sir say,

"Come on, back to work," though I bet everybody is thinking about the skeletons that have been found, wondering how they died.

Soon he has us writing about it, trust him, and talking on tape, giving our ideas on the subject, so that we can do a school news sheet, asking who we think the skeletons might have been when they were alive, and why the cellar was closed like that (that is if you want to, some kids say it gives them the screaming eeble jeebles just to think about it at all). But when I take my story up to Sir, ten pages of it, plus illustrations, ready

70

to do it up on tape and slides, he says it's the best thing I've ever done and congratulations.

"It's my sort of subject, that's why," I explain.

"Unfortunately I cannot find skeletons every day in order to give you inspiration," he grins.

At times, I can see why he's got a giant-sized fan club in this school. But he's still a teacher and they're berks, sub-human.

At the end of the morning, waiting to be called for dinner, everyone stands jabbering, Rosie and my face forgotten.

"I wonder if it will be in the papers," says Helen Lockey.

"We might be on telly," squeaks Tracy.

"They won't let us near the place," says Simon Singh. "I just been now to take a dekko and they've put a fence around and a notice to say how forbidden it is to enter."

"Oh, they never let us have any fun. I should have liked to explore down there," says JJ.

Coming from the well-known coward, this strikes me as very funny.

"It's easy enough to go down there if you really want to," I say.

"I'd be scared," shivers Heather, looking like a jelly-bellied rhino, "with all the ghosties and bats and spiders and rats down there."

"I don't think any school cellar can be very scary."

"Oh, you're just boasting, Corby," sneers JJ. "You'd be dead scared. Why, when we jumped you, you cried and pretended to be dead. . . ."

"Shut up," snaps Stewpid. "We ain't talking about that."

Rosie, who has been very quiet, listening to all this, now shows her brace in a toothy grin.

"A whole team on to one person makes anybody play dead. They would be very stupid not to do so."

"You don't know anything about it," JJ snaps. "You've only just come to this school, so you shouldn't go shoving your nose into things you know nothin' about. What I am saying is that Corby is too chicken to go down that cellar, although he says it's easy."

"Pack it in," says Stewpid. "Let's leave it, shall we?"

"You talk a whole load of crap, anyway," I say to JJ. "I don't care whether I go down the cellar or not, it's nothing to me one way or another, all I say is, that if anyone wants to, it's easy."

Mrs. Bond, the dinner lady, starts to line us up.

"However much you boast, I *know* you're chicken," hisses JJ at me.

"Quiet, everybody," cries Mrs. Bond.

"I'll go down there, any time."

"I don't believe you."

"Get knotted, little boy."

"Are you talking to me?" He squares up, fists clenched, and I start to laugh, for he looks very funny.

"Sorry, but you need the rest of the team before you even look like one fighter. . . ."

"Chicken. Chicken." He licks his lips. He's gone barmy.

"Quiet, over there," sings out Mrs. Bond.

"When do I go?"

"Today. Before they close it up."

"O.K."

"You have to bring something out to prove you've been in there, else I shan't believe you."

"Fine. I'll do that small thing."

"You're mad," says Stewpid. "Both of you."

"You're fine, Count Dracula," says Rosie.

"I still say you're chicken," JJ grinds on.

"Look, if I do this, get this idiot off my back for me," I ask Stewpid.

"I'm keeping out of this," says Stewpid. "I've got the team to worry about. The doctor says I can play again next week."

Dinner is meatballs and rice, followed by ginger pud. I sit by Rosie, and instead of giving Heather a bit of fun which is what I usually do at dinner-time, Rosie and I plan strategy. I have to keep out of sight of Buggsy and the workmen. And see that JJ doesn't tell tales to somebody, so Rosie says she'll stick to him like glue. Dinner over, I wander round to the forbidden area, and sure enough it's knocking off time, half of the workmen aren't there, and the rest are drinking their tea in the tin hut.

I run to the playground tree, and flatten myself against it, then run from there to the hole, like Starsky and Hutch. The blank gaping hole welcomes me. The fence is nothing, it wouldn't stop a flea, let alone me.

It's dark inside, just as I thought it would be. First I jump down the stairs that have been boarded up for years, run swiftly down and turn out of sight from the world above. Here it's plenty dark, with no movement or sound at all, the only light a sliver from that opened up bit where I came in. The air smells stuffy and thick as I move forward slowly, hands out in front, ready to encounter trouble, ready to protect myself from anything at all that may be lurking, anything that may have stayed down there from when it had all been first locked up, all those years ago. And for the first time I really do wonder why it was locked up, what for? And I shiver a bit, but not much, for the dark's my friend, and has been for a long time now. Only, I wish Boris was with me. Boris is usually with me when I go exploring in the dark. His whiskers twitch beside me. But here I am alone. And I can't help wondering, as I move slowly forward, if the cellar was boarded up because it wasn't safe, or because something had to be boarded up down here because it was ... dangerous ... and those thoughts are dangerous so I push them away and watch carefully what I am doing.

I'm getting used to the dark now, and can see much better. The room is large, with a low ceiling above, and a grating at the far end, so bunged up with dirt and cobwebs that only a pale ray of light straggles through. The floor is stone, uneven and dirty. In the corner are a couple of old desks with iron feet and lift-up lids and seats, like the ones they had in schools long ago, with a pile of clothes on the floor beside them. I stir the clothes with my feet as there might just be a ratty friend there, a cousin of Boris. But nothing is in the clothes nor in the desks when I peep inside, only an old smell that seems as if it gathers up and moves away, and a fat spider scuttling into the distance. "I shan't hurt you," I tell it.

I turn to the corner with the arch Sir spoke of. There it is in the gloom, rounded above the rubble, but there

74

are no white bones, no skeletons. They've gone. Pity. I should've liked to see those. It is all quiet and sad, somehow. I look around for something to take back, there's an empty inkwell in the desk—they must have had fun throwing ink at each other in the old days—I take one, and there's a scrubbing brush with half its bristles missing, a broken globe, and an old clock with Roman numerals, stopped at twelve o'clock. Midday? Midnight? I stop and listen as something stirs on the edge of my hearing and is gone again. I'd better get a move on. The tea break will be over soon, and I must get out of here. As I turn to go a small cupboard catches my eye. I open the door. It is empty, except . . . except for a key, old, ordinary. I pick it up and push it into my pocket and close the door. Then I turn to leave.

And for a minute I do not know where to get out of the cellar.

And I am afraid, terrified, I have the feeling that the cellar does not want me to go, it wants to keep me for company in its age-long loneliness, and I am so scared I break out in a sweat, despite the fact that it is autumn and cold underground, and my heart is pounding so loud that I can't think, think, think, go on, think, you know the way out of here, it's quite light really, then where has the entrance gone?

And it's there, just where it was all the time, and I don't know why I was afraid, after all, I like the dark and I like cellars, I'm used to them, let's get out of here, fast, Gowie, you've done what you said you'd do and you've got something to prove it, let's go, go. . . .

I head for the great outside, and straight into Buggsy, who just by chance is waiting by the tree. . . .

"Funny it should be you," he says. "Come on, let's go and visit the Headmaster."

He stands me in front of a large notice saying,

ALL CHILDREN MUST STAY AWAY FROM THIS AREA. IT IS DANGEROUS.

"Pity you never learned to read," he says.

I have to write out two hundred words beginning with B, and their meanings. I know quite a lot of rude words beginning with B, but I'm not allowed to use *them*. Rosie slips in to help me with a few. She is bothered because JJ managed to get away from her trailing him, when he went to the bogs. She thinks he came out the other side and then told Buggsy I was in the cellar.

I'm not bothered. At the end of the afternoon, nearly everyone from all the fourth year comes to look at the key and the inkwell, and I give a talk, describing the cellar and How I Felt in There. JJ walks away looking green and stupid, as the crowd gathers round.

Only at the end do I see Sir detach himself from a corner and walk away, as well. He's carrying the cassette recorder.

"Makes a good tape," he grins. "Thanks, Corby."

Chapter 8

"Draw a snake on a dead man's back,
Chop off his head and who did that?"

One evening, not long before Hallowe'en, we are coming back home through the fields above the valley on the edge of the city. I've taken Rosie to Stoke Woods to gather chestnuts, which she has never done before. It is starting to get dark and we are hurrying home. Thunder-grey clouds swirl in the sky and the trees glow yellow and red, except where they've felled those dead or dying from Dutch Elm disease. Barbed wire is nailed up across the valley so that you can't run straight down to the stream any more. Trees lie everywhere, nettles and thistles stand in huge clumps.

Rosie is in front, and I am running with Boris in my hand, he enjoys an outing, when, suddenly, as if at a signal, rooks fly over the valley, a great black cloud, hundreds and hundreds and hundreds of them, I have never seen so many, turning and wheeling, wave after wave, till the sky is black wings, then they fly silently on past the bare black branches of the dead trees at the end of the valley.

And I feel as if something wonderful and tremendous is about to happen and there is the feeling inside me that I shall burst. And I know from the way Rosie is watching that she feels it too, so,

"Get a move on," I yell. "Don't just stand there. You look spastic."

And she turns and grins and we race home in silence, coming into the smell of eggs and beefburgers and chips, and what she calls cookies, with Rosie's mum all smiles and welcome, and Rosie's little brother, Joe, aged two, following me like a puppy dog, wanting to wrestle. I ain't known a really little kid before, he scared me at first, but he just grins at me all the time and thinks I'm the bee's knees. The room is warm and full of people and food, and afterwards we watch *Dr. Who*.

And I'm happy.

Only, part of me wants to be out there still, where the birds toss and fly, weaving strange circles in their cold, wild world of air and sky.

Tom has babies, and Miss is astonished just as I thought she would be, but very pleased, you'd think she'd done it all herself. There are ten babies, and Miss takes them home with her for a week so that they will be quiet and mad Momma Tom won't be tempted to eat them. She just might.

On Wednesday we sit in front of work cards that read: —

PAPIER-MACHE PUPPETS

1. Make a head out of plasticine, taking care to form strong features and a thick neck.
2. Smear vaseline over the head.
3. Mix flour paste in a bucket. Dip small pieces of torn

newsprint into it. Cover head with as many layers as possible, the more the better. Leave to dry.

4. Slice head open with Stanley knife. Plasticine should fall out easily. Stick head back together with paper and paste. Leave to dry.

5. With thick powder paint cover head with white or neutral base. Leave to dry.

6. Paint features, add hair, etc. Leave to dry.

7. Sew dress, with hands.

8. Stick dress to neck of puppet with Bostic.

9. Write or make up a play with a group.

10. Get ready to perform it in the puppet theatre.

Count Dracula, I croon to myself as I shape the well loved features. Rosie is creating a ghost. We have chosen our materials, white sheeting for the ghost, black velvet, perfect for the Count. There was only a bit left, but I've found that Miss Plum lets me have nearly any-thing if I smile my Tom smile at her. All we have to do this afternoon is model the head, and tear up loads of paper and soak it in the buckets with flour paste. Half the class is doing this, while others are creating a frieze on the wall, a witch whizzing over the roof-tops, real twigs in her broom, spiders and bats out of pipe cleaners and cotton wool hanging in corners. We've written eerie poems and decorated them and these are up on the wall, Darren's is a spook riddle, and really good. We've moved the little wooden puppet theatre into the classroom, ready for rehearsals. The afternoon goes quickly.

"You are *good* these days," says Helen Lockey, as we shred paper together.

"I am a *saint*. I always was, but no one is pestering me."

JJ is away. With flu, they say. I hope it's lethal.

"He may die in great pain," I say, hopefully.

"You're not supposed to say that sort of thing," says Rosie. "Even if you think it."

"I'm thinking of something else."

"What?"

"I'm hoping that Heather may knock that bucket of paste all over her dirty great feet."

And before Rosie can say sh, there is the gran and grandad of all wails from the Activity area, where Heather has just knocked the bucket of paste over her flippin' great boats. . . .

Rosie and me, we stare at each other. . . .

"It's the power, Count Dracula . . . it's the power," she whispers.

At about half-past six that night I start to feel starving and there not being a sausage in the fridge except Jamaica Rum ice cream, three packets, all of which I finish, I decide to get some Chinese food from the Takeaway. I like Indian grub better but I'd already had curry, my Mum had left me one of those Vesta packets and some money on the mantelpiece in case I wanted any more. She's been in a good mood just lately. Anyway, when I get outside, Mouse Adams, Peter Tawnay and Rod Gillett are all there, heaped on their Hondas, and making witty comments about my face which is healing now, though I still look like a rainbow on legs. They're friends of my brother Mark, and they're trouble. Mouse thumps me matily, and I grin as if I like it, because it doesn't pay to get on the wrong side of Mouse, it just isn't worth it, the result always being painful in some way. I stand with them and eat my takeaway, all the time wanting to get back to the telly and Boris in peace, and eat my grub on my lonesome.

They ask about Mark and when he's coming home.

"He's all right. Out soon. Forget when."

The bikes rev up and explode into the night.

I am just back inside when Rosie arrives to ask me if I'll go back with her to school as she's forgotten her homework, and maybe there is still a possibility of getting into school to fetch it.

"Whadya want to do homework for?" I ask as we walk along in the growing dark. "I don't believe in it."

"It's my mother. She's hung up on this women's equality thing. She intends me to become a doctor, so I have to do plenty of work if I'm gonna qualify."

"Good. You can save some spare corpses for me. I expect you'll get plenty . . . hey, that hurt. . . ."

She chases me down the road, but I'm quicker even if she's bigger than me.

Buggsy hasn't gone because they have a meeting on at school, he tells us.

"Straight in and out. Don't mess about," he says.

We go into the classroom and Rosie picks up the books she needs.

"Your Maths is better than mine, anyway," she says, "so you don't need to worry."

"I don't. Neither does anyone else. Nobody gives a frozen sausage whether I do my work or not."

"Hurry up now," calls out Buggsy. "Go the other way

81

out, not out of the front. It's dangerous that way, with the cellar not properly filled up yet."

We walk through the school. It echoes as we go.

"I don't like it much. It frightens me," says Rosie. "Schools at night are real scary."

The witches painted by the third year watch us as we go through their classroom. Somewhere people are talking, and Rosie and Buggsy are coming behind me, but they seem far away, as if we're separated by a wall of glass. I get to where the door to the playground should be, a door I've been in and out of since I was a little kid, and it's gone. And I feel strange and sick, as if nothing is real at all, and the whole school is changing around me into something different.

I'm scared.

"The builders have shifted the door," says Buggsy. "It looks funny, doesn't it, over there. I can't get used to it. Now, get along home. And don't forget your things next time, or I shan't let you in. I wouldn't have let him in," he says to Rosie. "Not on his own. Never know what you'll be up to, do we?" he says to me. I don't care. I've only just stopped feeling sick, and wouldn't care if I never went into school again as long as I live.

In a minute we are runnning down the road and back home until we stop, out of breath.

"You were scared in there. Why?"

I was going to say no I wasn't, she was imagining things, but that's a waste of time with Rosie, she likes to dig into the middle of things where there are no skins left, so I tell her I don't know, that it's a feeling of things being unreal, and it frightens me very much, and just now school seemed as if it wasn't there on this planet at all but somewhere else and me with it. You don't think I'm goin' bananas, I ask her, and she says no, I'm one of the most unfruity people she's ever met and we get a fit of the giggles, so I don't tell her that there's something else I've been thinking about as well, which is bothering me. We go into her house and Joe has his bath, and he is being very naughty his mother says and she is glad to see us, so I give him piggy backs and flies in the air and he laughs so much we both fall on the floor and the little key that is in my pocket falls out.

"You are still keeping this little ole key," Rosie says, picking it up, and once again I am going to tell her, but I wait till Joe has gone to bed and we go round to my house, when she has done her homework.

"Rosie," I say, at last, and very cautiously, as I do not wish to have someone fall about at what I am going to say, however barmy it sounds.

"Mm," she answers, and she is stroking Boris on her lap.

"You know when the bucket went over Heather?"

"Mm."

"Oh, listen."

"I'm listening."

"Well, it was the power from this key. The one I found."

"How do you know?"

"It's not the only time."

"What else has happened?"

"JJ caught the flu, when I willed it on him."

"That would have happened anyway."

"Oh, I know. But then, there've been little things like

getting the lessons I want, or wanting someone to fall over, and my favourite football team winning last Saturday, and willing there to be twenty pence in the bowl on the mantelpiece and there was, and wishing for Jamaica Rum ice cream for tea and there was. You know."

"No, I don't. It just sounds weird. Like in stories. Like Aladdin. You don't rub the key, do you?"

"No. I just sort of will things."

"Do it now."

"What?"

"I don't know. I can't think of anything. Wait a minute. Yeah. Let's wish for some chocolate biscuits in the tin, instead of those plain ones which were in there when I looked a minute ago."

"Abracadabra. I wish there were some chocolate biscuits in that tin over there," I say, feeling a complete twit. We give the tin a minute and then peer into it. The dreary-looking plain biscuits haven't changed one bit for the better.

"That's that, then. I'm glad it was all in your mind, Gowie."

"So am I," I reply, lying.

"Yes, you had me worried for a minute." She stood up to go, yawning and stretching. "I'm sorry life's not magic, like in books, but perhaps it's safer. You never know what dangerous things might happen with all that magic around. Got to go. See you, Count Dracula."

"See you."

She pushes open the door just as Belinda, her sister, is coming the other way.

"What do you want?"

"Ma says would you like to come and have some milk shake and orange chocolate biscuits with us, Gowie. They're a new sort and kinda del-ish-ous."

"Oh, oh, oh," cries Rosie. "Count Dracula strikes again."

"Stop talking rubbish," says her sister.

Later that evening I lie on the floor with Boris running over me and think how my life has changed since Rosie Lee found me in the doorway, and how there are lots of super things to do like the puppets, and how Rosie's family are going to take me to Cornwall with them, and how I'm sure I'm special, that I've got a special magic gift. And Boris grins his ratty grin at me to show he's magic as well, and I give him a really loving stroke, because he was once my only friend, and he's still my oldest one.

Chapter 9

"I am cold and alone...."
E. J. SCOVELL

These days I wake up in the morning really looking forward to school and that's because I'm enjoying making my puppet. It's coming on really well, as I pile on layer upon layer of wet sticky newspaper, shaping and smoothing till paste oozes everywhere. It takes time, for you need a lot of layers. But, at last, I think I've done enough and I dry out the head on a tray on the radiator. Then Miss cuts the head for me with a Stanley knife, I don't like this bit much, I feel that I shall hear a scream coming from him, but the plasticine comes out like a ripe conker from its shell. The papier-mâché is several layers thick, and it sticks back together easily. And the good bit, painting the face, dead white to begin, then leave it to dry, then the black eyes and red dripping mouth and the fangs, and black wool for hair. While it's drying, Miss Plum helps me to sew his velvet cloak, which isn't easy, but looks fantastic, with white felt hands sewn to the ends of the seams, with red talons on them. As we sew I work out a scenario with Rosie and Darren. And it's good.

JJ is still absent.

Rosie is starting violin lessons that evening, which makes me fall about to think of her screeching away.

"You'd be better if you played a musical instrument," she says. "It would relieve some of your tensions and neuroses, then you wouldn't need to be so aggressive." She talks like this at times. "Hey, why don't you take up the guitar or the drums? That would suit you."

I can't stop laughing. "I don't need musical instruments. I just need to be able to duff in all my enemies, then I shouldn't have any problems."

"Fighting and violence never solved any problems. And you have to sort yourself out before you can sort out other people—"

"But you're trying to sort *me* out before you've got yourself sorted out with these violin lessons you're just about to start—"

"You win, Count Dracula. Still, I'm not having you laugh at my music even if I do make the most god-damned awful noise to begin with. . . ."

"That's enough of that shocking language, Rosie Angela Lee," cries her mother from the kitchen. "I never hear Gowie using language like that, and I don't want to hear it from your lips, or I shall wash out your mouth with carbolic."

Rosie's Mum is pretty strict. I grin smugly at Rosie, who kicks me on one ankle, and mutters, "Creep."

"Your Mum thinks I'm good."

"You are really. You just try hard to be bad, but you've never fooled me."

"Wait and see, when the moon is at the full, I shall turn into a werewolf."

"More like a were-teddy bear."

That really is enough, so I give her a half-nelson, till she begs for mercy, and Mrs. Lee comes in.

"It'll be dark when Rosie finishes, and it's a long distance from here to Mrs. Bates, who's giving the lesson. I can't meet you, Rosie, because I've got my Literature Class tonight, and your father is looking after the little ones. Will you be all right?"

"I'll meet her, Mrs. Lee."

"Oh, you are a good boy," she repeats, and I smile my Tom smile. She finds me a bar of chocolate as a result.

"Rosie's afraid of the dark, you know," says her mother to me, while Rosie is changing into her jeans. "And she doesn't like people to know."

"I think everybody's a bit afraid of it. Only I've got used to it."

"Yes, but she's more frightened than my other children. She had to have a night light when she was little."

"I don't think Joe's afraid of anything," I say as he bangs my knees with his head, so that I will give him a piggy-back.

Later I collect Rosie from her lesson.

"You do look nutty with that case."

"I don't mind looking nutty. It does not bother me one little bit. I am not one of your conventional girls, and if you are ashamed to be seen with me and my violin case you didn't have to meet me. I'm a girl. I can look after myself."

"I had to come in case you got mugged, though who would take you on with that brace I don't know."

"Gowie Corby, I'll. . . ."

"Don't bother to hit me. The other reason is I know you are scared of the dark, 'cos your mother told me, just now."

"She tells all my secrets," complains Rosie. "She uses me as a kind of conversation starter with people. *Do you know my daughter, Rosie Angela, she stands on her head eight times a day, wearing her pyjamas and waggling her big toes. Do you find that interesting, Mrs. Pudding? Do any of your children exhibit similar tendencies?* Why can't she have things of her own to talk about, her doings, and not use me? I don't talk about her, much."

"Hey, don't get mad. At least, she does care about you."

"I wish she'd forget I was there, sometimes."

"I think your Mum is nice, so there. Anyway, you have to put up with her like I have to put up with mine."

We walk on in silence. Rosie does not seem happy.

"What's up?"

"Oh, my throat is a little sore, and I have a headache 'cos I was nervous about my violin class, but it was fine, and I worry about things because I think my mother expects me to be cleverer than I am, and uphold the cause of Women's Liberation for her."

"You're all right. It's just you come out with things English children don't say, and you use longer words."

"You mean I am more articulate, and analyse things more than you do."

"Yeh, I suppose that's what I mean."

"But I can't write as well as you English kids. I couldn't write stuff like Darren does—"

"He's a genius anyway."

"I can't do Maths as well as you can. That's why I have homework."

"Don't worry. Soon we'll be dead, anyway."

"What I really wanted to talk to you about, though not in school, was your gift."

"My what?"

"Your gift. Making things happen."

"Oh, that. It only happens sometimes and then it's probably a coincidence."

"That's what I wondered about. Suppose. Suppose we tried to wish, or you tried to make something big happen. Not chocolate biscuits, something like making the school fall down."

"Smashin' idea. No school tomorrow. No more school and sorrow. Except they'd put up another one, pretty fast, I bet, the meanies."

"Shall we do it? You do it?"

"If we make the school fall down, we'll kill Buggsy and the cleaners who are in there, right now."

"Well, we'll wait till eight o'clock. It should be empty by then."

So, at eight, solemnly, I hold the key in my hand and wish for the school to fall down. We decide we won't have any other wishes, so as to keep loads of power for this big one.

And outside, there sounds the most tremendous roar. Rosie shoots half a mile into the air, crying, "What was that?"

90

"Only Mouse Adams's gang living it up. Nuthin' to worry about."

"I don't like them."

"Oh, Mouse is all right. He's never done me any harm."

"I still don't like them. They're menacing. Besides, I thought it was the key answering back. Or the school falling down."

But school is still there next day. There in the bloomin' awful pouring rain, which means there'll be no football that afternoon, and I still like the afternoon football even if I'm not in the team. What's more, Rosie's sore throat is much worse and she's got to stay in bed.

Rosie is away. JJ is back.

The morning is long and draggy and boring. I get half my Maths wrong and have to do it again, and Miss Plum tears a page out of my English book 'cos it's so untidy, and I just can't be bothered to turn on my Tom smile. The radio programme we have on Thursday must have been written by morons with the most awful snobby accents you've ever heard, and I get told off for drawing swastikas over my pamphlet. The end of the morning arrives after several thousand years, and after Haricot Stew, Haricot Spew would be a better name for it, and Prune Pudd, we have to go back to the classrooms because it's still sending down stair rods outside, the chess club is cancelled, and so are most of the other clubs, because a lot of the teachers are absent with flu. So I go to the Activity area to look at my puppet, the one bright spot in a black day.

It's lying smashed on the floor. JJ is just moving away from it.

And my inside hurts as though someone has pushed a knife into my guts. Miss Plum is standing there, suddenly.

"Don't mind so much, Gowie. GOWIE!"

But I've gone. Past her, after him, into the drama area, through the cloakroom, hard behind him as he runs. And part of me can see me running and the faces turning to watch, and the terrified face of JJ turning round to see if I am coming. And, brother, I am. I am coming to settle you for ever. I knock Heather out of the way, she falls screaming to the ground, and JJ runs out of the classroom into the cloakroom, and into the boys' new bog, where I have him, trapped, he can't get away, and I thump hell into him, so that he cries and bends and tries to protect himself, and leaps on to the cistern in a frantic effort to escape.

The top part cracks, breaks and drops to the floor in pieces. The new cistern. And I am quite suddenly calm as he stands shivering in front of me, looking at the wrecked cistern.

"Corby," says a voice behind me.

"It's all right, Mr. Merchant. I'm coming."

Jonathan Johns and I stand before the headmaster. He looks cold and old.

"I am writing to your parents," he is saying. "They will have to pay for the damage. This kind of vandalism cannot be allowed to go unpunished."

JJ is crying. I stare at the rain pouring outside and the *Doctor Who* plant.

92

"I am going to cane you, now," the Head continues. "You will receive three strokes on each hand and then I shall write down what I have done in the punishment book. It is a long time since I wrote anything in there, because this is part of my task as a Headmaster that I do not enjoy. But damaging property that has only just been installed at considerable expense cannot be permitted. You are boys in the top class of the school and others follow your example."

His voice is steady and calm and seems to come from a long way away. I do not feel that I am really there. This is not happening. I try not to think what my mother will say when she is asked to pay for the damage. I try not to think of the pain of the cane.

I think of Rosie and I wish that it hadn't happened, that the cistern wasn't broken, that JJ hadn't come back, that my puppet, my puppet wasn't broken, that it was yesterday and I was laughing with Rosie, that the school had fallen down last night at eight o'clock when I wished it had.

But I am still standing in front of the Headmaster in his study on a rainy day, and he is bending the cane, testing it before he hits my hands.

There is no magic, and no Rosie to cry if I am hurt. I knew there was no magic, really, all the time, even when we were pretending I could will things to happen with the help of the key.

The Headmaster canes JJ first. He weeps and blubbers and leaves crying his eyes out.

The Headmaster looks sadly at me, his eyes blue and far away.

"I've known many boys," he says, "and I've caned

some of them. You are stranger than most of them. I do know it's hard for you, you know. I had hoped, lately. . . . But here you are again. It's very sad. You see, Gowie Corby, soon it will be too late, and if you go on the way you are now, you will land in prison, and that will be a waste, a terrible waste."

I think of the key and wish, don't let him cane me, don't let him cane me, DON'T LET HIM CANE ME. Then as in a nightmare I hold out my hand, the cane whooshes, it hurts, it hurts. I don't cry. He looks at me. Is he waiting for the tears?

"Corby, did that hurt?"

"Yes, Sir. On the outside, Sir."

He puts down the cane.

"Not an inside hurt. Not like. . . ?" He watches me.

I look away. I don't want to know. I don't want to be conned again, like Merchant cons me into telling things I don't want to say. Yet I do say.

"Not like with Joe. When he was dead, and my mother wouldn't stop screaming. Or seeing my puppet broken. Sir."

"Go away, boy. Try to keep out of trouble. Where's that girl, today?"

"She's away, Sir. With a sore throat."

"Stay with her and away from that boy and you might get through the year. Go now, Corby."

"Sir. Aren't you gonna cane me, any more?"

We look at one another, then he says,

"There isn't much point."

"Thank you, Sir." I wait, then—

"I did break the cistern, Sir. And my mother won't pay the money."

94

"You want to be caned."

"No. But I don't want not to be."

The blows are sharp and swift. I cry as I leave the headmaster's study. Only, I'm crying for a lot of things that have nothing to do with having hands that hurt.

Chapter 10

Tonight's the night, a very fine night,
I hope there'll be no ghosts tonight.

Rosie comes back to school, and she seems to have grown even bigger and be more full of energy, and she starts organising the class for an American thing she calls Trick or Treat. I thought she called it Trickle Treat at first and couldn't make out what the heck she was jabbering about, but it turns out to be Trick or Treat, which is a fine ole American custom. An' Rosie is keen on carrying on this fine ole American custom over here in this fine ole British neighbourhood. The kids all laugh at her at first, but the thing about Rosie is that she doesn't mind, she just laughs back with 'em and the next thing you know she's getting everybody to do what she wants. She sits on a table explaining and waving her legs about, and soon dozens of kids—not all from our class—are promising to turn up at her house at five-thirty on Hallowe'en night, that is tomorrow, wearing fancy dress or a mask, both if poss., and carrying a carrier bag to put candy and cookies in, no she says quickly, she means cakes and sweets, which the people will give to the kids who knock on the door and ask for Trick or Treat. If you are refused you put soap on their

96

window or rubbish on the doorstep—that will get you into trouble quicker than anything says Helen Lockey— and Rosie replies that she's already thought of that and she's got a whole lot of stuff ready, notices to be given out mainly to the parents of kids at school or known to be friendly, saying that the TrickorTreaters are coming, and will they be very, very kind and have a small something ready. And she's made stickers with Meanie on it to put on the doors of those people who do not fancy handing out sweets to a lot of kids dressed up to look spookie on their doorsteps. She is sure this will be a success and there'll be enough goodies at the end for a feast at her house, her mother is letting her have the front room. And tell your folks that we shall stick together in case of muggers and so on, she adds.

"And nasty old men," says Heather.

"Any one who goes for you needs a new guide dog," I put in there, and am told to hush.

Somebody points out that this ole British neighbourhood is not rich like America and may not wish to give away loads of sweets to kids like us, and they also may be saving for Bonfire Night which is due soon. In reply, Rosie says that all Americans aren't rich, anyway her family aren't but they always give something for Trick or Treat, which is a much less dangerous celebration than Guy Fawkes night, and so they should be pleased. Just think—here she stands up on the table—I may not be here for long, and I should so much like to do this with you. And kid brothers and sisters will be welcome, too, she adds as an afterthought.

JJ there remarks that he's glad to hear she's going and the sooner the better as far as the *Team* are concerned. The team are standing gloomily on the edge of the crowd of kids gathered round Rosie.

"We can do without you, nasty nerk that you are," snaps Rosie. "We don't want your sort of violence, thank you."

Rosie is trying very hard to talk like us and she comes out with very funny sayings at times. And now everybody falls about with laughing at JJ, who does a cherry and stalks off, followed by Stewpid and some others. Nasty nerk becomes a school saying in no time, and the second year make Nasty Nerk cardboard badges and sell them at a penny each, that's Graham Chambers, he's always making money, last year he made thirty-seven quid just showing his old moth-eaten panda in a push-chair and asking for a penny for the guy. He's little, with curls, and people give him money like there are no tomorrows. He can't read, but he says you don't need to. He's got over a hundred nicker stashed away.

Anyway, Rosie gets lots of promises from people to turn up, and lots of people to deliver her notices.

Now the thought of this Trickle Treat business is filling me with a certain deep uneasiness, and I talk to Rosie during the afternoon, when I am once more creating a Count Dracula, with Miss Plum on the other side of me doing most of the work because she was so upset about the other one, which suits me fine, and I am sitting like an angel between them and Sir comes past and grins, saying:

"You are getting spoilt, Gowie Corby. You'll end up as a goody, yet."

"Never, Sir, I'll always be with the baddies," I answer, and then turn to Rosie and tell her she is strain-

98

ing our friendship somewhat, and if I sound like that it is because we are starting to talk like Rosie just as she is beginning to talk like us.

"What's the matter, Count?" she asks.

"I am not at all sure that I wish to be found on our street at night dressed in some horrible outfit shouting Trickle Treat and having some old dear have a heart attack, or fetch her old man with a shot gun, because she knows my Dad and thinks I am following in his footsteps going in for armed robbery. . . ."

I sink down filled with gloom.

"I do get your point though I think you may be worrying unnecessarily," Rosie replies.

"Gowie, you don't mean it. Your Dad didn't really go in for armed robbery, did he?" says Miss Plum, opening her eyes very round and wide.

"Oh, yes," I say. "I thought you knew. Of course, I don't like boasting. . . ."

"Boasting!" she echoes in a sort of weak voice.

"Yeh, it sounds like boasting if you say your old man was a terror. But he was. Once he went into a jeweller's and walked off with a tray off the counter and nobody stopped him because he looked as if he was supposed to be doing it. He said you could get away with anything if you put up a sign saying PUBLIC WORKS or something. People don't like to interfere, he said."

"But that isn't *armed* robbery."

"No, my Mum used to say she didn't mind that sort of thing, it was when he got one of his nasty fits and beat us all up that she got stroppy. Then Joe got big and could stop him, but after Joe got killed, he got worse, then one day he came in absolutely legless—sorry

Miss—and he'd been with a dolly bird in the pub, and my Mum waited till he went in the bog, then she beat him about the head with a broom and threw him out and he went off with the dolly bird, and fell in with a gang, and they beat up this couple that kept a shop, down in Torquay, and I think he was mixed up with some betting gang as well. He got seven years. My mother says she's glad but she misses him. Her boy friend's not up to much. Layabout Larry they call him. Sorry, Miss."

"Gowie." Miss Plum swallows a bit.

"I miss him as well."

"How can you miss him, Gowie? A man like that. You must feel happier with him away, safely away."

"No, he told me jokes, and played football with me. Sometimes. And he remembered birthdays and pocket money. My Mum forgets, or doesn't want to remember."

Miss Plum is sitting silent, and suddenly I wish I hadn't talked so much about my old man.

"I didn't mean to go talking like that ... it's not right, is it, you being a teacher and all that. . . ."

She takes hold of my hand, which makes Rosie grin and me do a cherry, which I hardly ever do.

"Gowie Corby," she says, "I think you teach me more than I do you. And now, it really is time to clear up for the end of the afternoon."

Lots of kids turn up for Rosie's Hallowe'en evening, and there's quite a good deal of interest stirred up in our fine ole British neighbourhood, just as Rosie hoped there would be. I cannot bear to knock and ask on doors

100

myself, but I turn up with a nylon stocking over my face and a machine gun and stand at the back guarding the rest, waiting in some way for trouble.

Sure enough after a time I see two sneaky dark figures on the other side of the road, skulking. The *Team* is either curious or jealous. I move over to keep an eye on them after I've alerted Rosie.

"If they cause trouble . . ." she says, eyes flashing.

Two little kids go up to a door, it's her gran one of them says, and they knock and say Trick or Treat and the old lady says,

"Eh, it's our Tracy. What do ee want, my lover?"

"A treat," announces Tracy, and says it's for Hallowe'en and so on.

"I'll see if I've got something for ee," says her gran and comes back with a couple of Mars bars, which the kids put in their bag with little ghouly cries and toddle back to Rosie on little ghouly feet, all excited with themselves. Now, I'm just thinking that I must have gone bananas standing here baby-minding on a cold night when I could have been watching telly, when I see the two sneaky figures, whom I identify as JJ and Pete Gillott, drop a whole load of rubbish on that same doorstep and then hop it round the corner. I investigate the rubbish and it consists of an old chicken carcase, some half-eaten fish and chips and a dry dog turd. No gran is gonna be pleased with that dumped on her doorstep. So I turn the corner and there crouched against the wall are my two enemies. I swing the gun on Gillott, hissing, "That's for rubbish," but JJ has leapt away, across the pavement, over the road, right in the headlights of a car driving up the street at that

101

moment, and I am just behind him, feet moving as if
there are power units in my shoes, and the car misses
me by inches, no, millimetres, as I bring down JJ in a
rugby tackle on the edge of the kerb. And he is completely at my mercy.

He starts to yell, "No, Corby, no. No."

And I let him get up. I don't know why. We stand
looking at one another.

"You nearly got me killed under that car just then,"
he says.

"You scum," I say. "I saw you. And what you did.
And I tell you what we're gonna do, now."

"What?" he mutters.

"You're coming back with me over the other side of
the road and you're gonna pick up all that rubbish you
put there."

"I didn't . . ." he begins, but I hit him, and he shuts
up.

"But I'll give you a bit of a chance. We'll have a bit
of fun. We'll wait for the next car, and then run across,
and if you dare be last across after me, I'll let you off
picking up the rubbish. I'll make somebody else do it,
instead."

He breathes heavily. "O.K.," he mutters at last. "But
you're mad, Gowie Corby," he says.

"I know, and I don't care, Jonathan Johns. There's
one coming now. Ready?"

We wait on the edge of the pavement. Every part of
me is alive, life is wonderful, terrific, I feel free, marvel-
lous, fantastic, super Gowie Corby. I can do anything,
be anything, life is a great and glorious game for me to
play and to win. My game. My world. My life. JJ sways

beside me. The air around us seems to sizzle, and he cannot bear it any longer and has run, and in a split second behind him I leap, fly, jump across the road. The breath of the car touches me as it roars past.

"I've won, JJ. And now, a little rubbish collecting, please. When you've picked it up, you can take it all the way down the road to the litter bin, and may you rot with it!"

Later we sit in Rosie's front room. Her Mum has made orange squash for everybody, and there's treats galore. After a bit somebody starts to sing "Mull of Kintyre" and "Old Macdonald had a Farm". Rosie sits there singing her head off, eyes shining, specs shining, teeth shining, brace shining, Rosie is happy. So I slip out Indian fashion to see Boris and watch a special ghost story for Hallowe'en that's on. After all, there's only so much of this good business that a sinner can stand.

But when they've gone she comes and rings on my door.

"I'm not coming in," she says, "as it's getting late, but I just wanted to say thanks very, very much, Gowie Corby, I surely do appreciate all you do for me, and if I hear of you playing Chicken across the road again, I'll ... I'LL ... never speak to you again, except to TELL YOU OFF!"

And who should come back to school but the little mice to a great reception. And they still have ten babies. Mad Momma Tom hasn't eaten any of them. Miss Plum is very pleased with them and herself. They all turn out to be grey, all ten of them, with no butter-coloured ones like Dad Jerry, which seems a bit of a pity, but they are lovely little things. We have to put extra chicken wire on the cage because the bars are rather far apart and they might escape. No, I haven't forgotten my plan, but I am waiting my own time to carry out my little scheme. In the meantime we make books about mice, and Miss reads us a book called *The Mouse and his Child*, and there's a villain in that story that I really like. He's called Manny Rat. Only he repents his ways at the end of the book and I think that's a bit out of character, as I don't like people who repent, and then I get to thinking that I'm a bit goody goody lately, so I put a rubber insect in Heather's shoe-bag, in her plimsoll, in fact, it's a particularly nasty-looking one, and she shrieks her head off when she puts her hand on it at P.E. time. I also let off a stink bomb in the boys' bogs, making them even smellier than usual. It's very nice watching JJ forcing himself not to tell everybody that it's me that did it, and it remains one of those great unsolved mysteries. It is quite hard telling Rosie that I didn't do it, oh, no, but I got better with a bit of practice.

Then one morning, Miss Plum comes in in a state of high excitement and concern, for she has heard on the news that children are being held as hostages in a school, abroad, in a primary school like ours. Some teachers are being held as well, and they are all in great danger. Miss Plum tells us that she identifies with them and that we could easily be in their place, and she would like us to write prayers for their safety, if we feel we are able to do so. I do not feel that I am able to do so, in that I do not feel it will make a blind bit of

104

difference, but I do not say so in case she is disappointed in my ideas about the whole business. However, I do write a long account of what I think would be the best methods of escaping from such a situation if it happens in our school. This works out quite well, and our only casualties are Heather and JJ and we have a funeral service over them afterwards. Stewpid is wounded. Sir does quite well, helping Rosie and me to save the whole situation, and I allow Miss Plum to be responsible for a truce with the terrorists. I do eighteen pages altogether, and Miss says she will read it at home, when she has the time. And the strength to read all that, Miss, I say, and she agrees.

Rosie doesn't write much. Only four lines. She has tears in her eyes as she writes them. Rosie cries at a sparrow losing half a feather. When Miss reads hers, she says, Oh, Rosie, and asks her to write it out very large and neat and put a pattern round it and it can go on the wall. Rosie concentrates hard as she's naturally a bit untidy, and in the end it goes up on the old school wall, that's still in our classroom where it hasn't been altered.

> God save the children big and small,
> God save the children short and tall,
> God save the children every one.
> God save them till the day is done.

At the top of it, she writes *Rosie's Prayer*.

Two days later the children are released by the terrorists.

Chapter 11

All in, all in, a bottle of gin,
All out, all out, a bottle of stout.

And there I am on the half-term holiday roaring along in the Lee mobile with Momma Lee at the wheel, driving as if she's at Brooklands, and Poppa Lee keeping the kids quiet, and not succeeding, for Joe keeps attacking me just for the hell of it, and Belinda keeps squabbling with everyone till she feels sick.

"She always feels sick," they all say, with no sympathy at all.

The car moves through the narrow lanes, where the beech leaves lie on the side of the road, at least Poppa Lee tells me they're beech leaves, but there are only two beeches I know, one with sand on it, and the other is gum, Beech Nut. It's good, too, only Rosie has cut down my ration, bossy bird that she is, and she's stopped me storing bits in my tray, etc., for later. Unhygienic, she says. Yanks are crazy about hygiene.

I have been to Cornwall before, but in Summer, cars nose to tail, petrol stink and boredom, waiting for Mum outside pubs, crisps and coke and boredom. Today Momma Lee has brought a basket full of grub, chicken and pizza and salad and peanuts, and everything you

106

can think of. And there's hardly anyone on the road except us. We end up at this little place called Morwenstow, just a house and a church and cliffs. There have never been such cliffs. The air is cool and damp. I send a pebble, it falls into the sea, creaming and curling miles below. We find a sheltered spot behind a rock for our picnic. For one who feels sick, Belinda manages to put away a surprising amount. Momma Lee reads us bits out of her guide book. She is a great one for information.

"The Vicar who lived here wrote poetry. Just fancy that, children. He sat in a hut on these cliffs and watched the seasons passing by and recorded what he felt about them. Isn't that just wonderful? Think of him sitting there and writing like that. You, with your sensitive and perceptive nature, Gowie, will surely appreciate that."

Rosie is making funny faces and rude noises, but her mother does not notice, which is just as well. Rosie's Mum always makes me out to be some sort of saint, nobody knows why, least of all me, but I like it, especially when it makes Rosie mad. Now, Joe seems bent on suicide and I have to keep hauling him back from the edge of the cliffs. We find the hut and sit inside on its wooden seat and gaze at the towering, crazy, technicoloured cliffs. And I think how queer it is that when we're in school the cliffs are still here, and the sea and the sky and sad, crying gulls. I should like to stay here for ever. No one could get at me. I'd be safe, safe for always. But if I can't stay here I want to take a piece of it back with me and keep it safe in my mind for ever, to take out and look at and be back here again, safe and good and right. Then suddenly, we all get up and run and run along the grass at the top of the cliff, with the wind stirring now, and tugging at us, and I think that everything will be right anyway, because it's different now, all different, everything changed.

Joe is tired and runs to me for a piggy-back, and we turn back to the car, for the wind is sharpening, it's starting to get dark, and it's nearly November.

Back in the car, there's grub and drinks, and we sing as Momma Lee tears homeward bound for Nelson Place.

The lights in my house are on, and Mum is back from her weekend, which I didn't expect.

"Come on," she shrieks. "You're late, and I want you to go to the off-licence. Come on, kid. Hurry up. We're going to celebrate."

A familiar figure, matchstick man, lounges behind her, pulling money out of his wallet, Larry Layabout. And behind him another figure.

"Hiya, kid. Wherja gedto, not in to welcome a guy home? Hello. What's here? A bird, eh?"

"Hi, Mark. This is Rosie. And her family. Rosie, this is my brother Mark."

"Rosie," Mark says, shaking with laughter. "That's a bloody funny name for a black bird, like you. Say, that's funny, black bird. Get it?"

"Yes. I've been getting it for years," Rosie answers. "And now, like the song, I'll say bye-bye. See you, Gowie."

We go in the house.

"You've got some peculiar friends," says Mark. "I

don't think much of your taste. Still, let's forget 'em. Whattle you have to drink, kid, since I'm back home?"

"Coke'll do."

"Right. Pleased to see me?"

And I look at him and see that he's grown, one helluva size. And if Mouse Adams looks like trouble, so does my brother Mark.

"Yeh, sure," I say.

Chapter 12

Iggly piggly poo,
Put the coward in your shoe,
When you're through let him go,
Inny tinny let him know.

My mother celebrates Mark coming out for about a week, then they have a terrific row, in which they throw things at one another and scream at the tops of their voices. I think they enjoy it, but I don't wait to hear much of it, shoot off rapidly into Rosie's, because I know that when they've finished with each other, they'll most likely turn on me. Mind you, when I hear Rosie screeching away on the violin, I think I've jumped out of the frying pan into the fire.

"You ain't 'alf torturing that poor cat," I yell.

"What cat?" she asks, actually stopping for a minute.

"The one whose guts you're sawing away at."

"Bah. You have no culture, you ignorant Gowie Corby."

At that moment, an especially loud yell and tremendous bang comes from my house next door, and Rosie jumps.

"What's that?"

"Oh, that's Mum and Mark showing the world there's no place like home."

"He won't hurt her, will he?" cries Rosie. "I must help her."

"Don't be funny. My Mum can deal with anything. Wait. Any moment now, there'll be a cry of pain, and she'll throw Mark out or push him out on the end of a broom."

We go and peer through the front-room window, and sure enough, after a time, Mark comes running out, shirt torn, hair standing on end, and the door slams shut behind him. He turns round and shakes his fist at it.

"What will he do now?" asks Rosie.

"Go down to the pub and get drunk, I expect. With Mouse and the gang."

"You are not to stop Rosie doing her practice," says Momma Lee, coming in. "You can help me put Joe to bed, as he's very naughty tonight, and then I shall show you how to play the piano. It's time you started to learn an instrument."

"Oh, no, not me," I cry, but after, when Joe is at last safely stowed away, I do have a go, and I find I quite like it, which is most astonishing. Back at home, I stay up late, sitting with Boris on my lap, watching the late night horror film, and it's a very good one, about a shuttered room and a mad female. Then Mark comes in and he's completely legless, but he hasn't brought all his mates back with him this time, which is one of the things that gets my mother mad with him, that and not trying to get a job. He's in a stroppy mood, as I thought he might be, saying he doesn't want to hang around in this dead-alive hole, and he's going to get some money

111

from somewhere and live it up. I've heard it all before and I'm enjoying the film, and so I don't take a lot of notice, until I realise that he's going on and on about Rosie being black, and how they shouldn't be living next door, and I shouldn't be having anything to do with 'em, and that he would tell Mum to put a stop to it, and they ought to go back to their own country, wherever that was, and he'd a good mind to give me a belting if I kept on going round to their house, rotten, lousy blacks.

In the end I get up without saying a word. The film has finished so I don't mind too much.

"Goodnight, Mark," I say, quiet-like, for I know he's plastered and it's no use arguing with him.

"Is that all you gotter say? I want you to promise me not to go near that girl again."

"You joking?"

"No, and I'll belt you round the ear'ole if you answer me like that."

"Night, Mark."

But he gets in between me and the stairs.

"Whatjer got to say?"

"I gotta say that that girl has been kinder to me than anybody in my whole life, and she makes me laugh, and she makes me feel good, so there." He is coming for me now, so I move fast. He's a bit slow, that's what got him nicked, before.

"You stop that black girl coming in here, or. . . ."

"Or what?"

"I'll tell Mum about that rat you've got in the cellar and we'll send it for vivisection. . . ."

"You do that, Mark Corby, and I'll kill you . . . I'll

112

kill you. . . ."

"You and who else?" he sneers, but he's cooling it, for he can see I mean it. I've shaken him. And I shall kill him, if he does anything to Rosie or Boris.

And my mother comes in with Layabout Larry.

"Get out, you two," she says, with great warmth and charm.

So we get out. At least we don't have to share a bedroom, as we did when Joe was alive. But Joe could deal with Mark. Joe was different. You can't trust Mark, no more than a rattlesnake. You never could. So, now I'll have to get Boris out of the cellar. I wish Mark had never come home. I wish he'd go away again. It was good before he turned up. And I fall asleep worrying about Boris.

At school, everybody is playing chicken. It's caught on.

Even the baby ghouls are daring each other to jump down the three steps leading to the first school. Older kids climb on to the flat part of the school roof above the cloakroom and dare each other to be the last to jump off before Buggsy catches them. Two boys have been sent to the Headmaster for climbing the tree in the school playground, and seeing who can jump off the highest branch. The house on the corner has had its doorbell rung so many times that the owner complained to the school, and the Headmaster has called in Sergeant Grant to give a talk on the dangers of Last Across, as the road is littered with bodies at times. I'm lying low, camouflage time, because I got problems enough at home without adding school ones to the list,

113

and anyway Rosie keeps her big brown optics on me. But I did offer Heather a Mars bar to kiss Stewpid, she'll do anything, sell her soul for a Mars bar. She waits till he's got the Team arranged in front of him while he gives a talk on tactics, then she totters up on her bandy legs and plants this smacker on his mush, and this turns out even funnier than I planned because she loses her balance, she's always losing her balance, that's because she's unbalanced, and falls sprawling over Stewpid, who topples the team like a bunch of skittles, 'cos he's a big lad, a big lad.

"Rape. Rape. Orgy. Orgy," I sing out at this moment. "I didn't know you fancied Heather, Stewp."

"I don't. I don't. I don't fancy anyone," he is shouting wildly, face red. I think he may be going to have a fit, but the whistle blows and he gains control.

"Well done," I say to Heather, giving her the Mars bar later. Little does she know that it's JJ's, he always has a good supply, and he gets upset when he finds her eating one, and his gone.

"Never mind, Heather," I say consolingly. "You can't help being a Mars bar kleptomaniac. You don't know you're taking them."

"But you gave it to me," she squeals. "For kissing Stewart."

"Your imagination does you proud," I say. "I don't know what you're talking about."

She tries to tell Miss, but she gets all streaky red and muddled, and I smile my Tom smile at Miss, and she doesn't believe her at all. Rosie comes back from the optician's then, so I am good. Rosie is always being fitted with teeth or specs or having feet straightened or some-

114

thing. Tonight we are moving the menagerie from my cellar to the shed at the bottom of Rosie's garden. Tonight we shall be busy. I don't want to move them out of my cellar, which I have cared for so much, but they aren't safe any more with Mark around, and the sinister figure of Mouse Adams hanging about all the time. I can't feel safe with them at all. Funny he should be called Mouse*, though. Momma Lee is very easy-going, and says provided that I keep them well cleaned out it's all right with her.

"She isn't easy-going with me, though," says Rosie, bitterly. "One and a half hour's homework plus violin practice now. She wants me to be a great woman when I grow up."

"You'll be that all right. Rosie Lee, biggest woman ever. Roll up, roll up, a pound to see the woman mountain. I'll make a fortune."

"Shut up, you," she says. Outside the rain pours down from a bad-tempered November sky, and inside the roar of pneumatic drills can be heard as a connection is tunnelled through to the cellar, which is going to be used for storage. It's a cheery sort of day. The Head, at Assembly, looking like the public hangman, and wearing his blackest suit, says that the present games must cease forthwith or severe penalties will be imposed—he talks like that in Assembly—and that extreme care must be exercised daily with the building works furnishing a hazard. I am happy thinking of how I shall make care do its exercises and what the opposite

*His real name's Maurice, which he never uses. Mouse is because of his teeth.

of forthwith might be (fifth-without?) when he astonishes everyone by saying that some foolish and unnamed child has fallen into the cement mixture. After that the school stays pretty quiet, except for the pneumatic drills. But we can't go outside, not with that rain, and somehow, in the jumpy atmosphere, rumours start flying around. So at dinner-time as we sit in the classroom, playing chess or draughts or hangman on the board, someone, I forget who, says that the school is definitely haunted, a ghost has been seen by one of the cleaners, staying late and discovering when she tried to get out that she couldn't find her way, as the school had changed back to what it was in Victorian times or even earlier, the school of 1665.

Yes, adds Tracy, they say the sounds of weeping have been heard and it's the cholera victims, and then the screams of those brought in wounded from the blitz, when the school became a hospital. Then Helen Lockey says that no, the school is haunted, but by that Saint, the one on the stained glass window in church, who walks through the school, dressed in a long white gown, stained with blood, and ... here she lowers her voice, and Heather makes a strange whiffling sound ... she is holding her head in her hand, and it's weeping, the head cut off by her ungrateful and unloving relatives, the peasants. There is a long silence at this, while the rain hammers down like steel rods, and the Hallowe'en witches, still up on the wall, grin down evilly at us. We look at each other, Rosie all eyes and teeth, and even the Team is silent, but not for long.

"The pneumatic drills have stopped," says Stewpid in a strange, strangled voice.

"It's dinner-time," croaks JJ.

This is a bit much, I feel, and as the well-known expert on vampires, werewolves and the supernatural, I make a joke.

Nobody laughs.

"I'm glad Gowie's here," quavers Heather. "He's the only one who's brave." And then,

"One thing, I'll say this for you, Corby, you may be a slob, but you've got guts." This is Stewpid speaking. I never did think he had much in his oversized head, but this is crazy.

But Rosie is looking at me as if I'm James Bond, the Hulk or Mohammed Ali.

"No, I haven't any guts at all," I say fast and furiously. "I'm a coward by nature, or by anything else."

"He's the only person I know who wouldn't be scared to stay in the school all night," says Heather.

Oh, no, no, no, no. Not with the headless one, thank you. Fancy holding a conversation with a head at knee height. No, thank you.

"Chief Sir said we'd got to stop playing dares and chicken. This would be the best one of all to finish up with." Has Helen Lockey gone completely round the twist? She's always been such a cool bird, with a neat cool voice and neat cool ways. What's she doing, stirring it?

"Go on, Corby," says Stewpid gruffly.

"No."

I want Rosie to say, don't do it, but she's still gazing soppily at me and murmuring something like good old Count Dracula.

And the well known voice, my favourite, chips in. JJ speaks.

"He won't. Gowie Corby's chicken. Gowie Corby's chicken."

"And yes, I am. And I don't care," I shout and Sir comes in.

Chapter 13

A whistle and a cry
Or let the game die.

But I am here at school, after all.

The little mice, Tom and Jerry and their babies, keep me company in the dark night, the little mice and a candle that I have placed a shade behind in the hope that it won't shine through the windows and bring in Buggsy or the Fuzz or anyone else that's curious about a candle shining through the window at school, late at night.

I didn't mean to be here. I don't mind being chicken, it doesn't bother me at all. I don't care about it. But Fate seems to have taken a hand and here I am, the doom feeling all about me.

After school Rosie and I, we start moving the cages from our cellar to their shed, and we work like stink, to get it all done before Mark comes back from wherever he's gone to. We carry through the gerbils and the mice and, last of all, Boris. We feed and settle them, and I show Boris round the shed so that he understands and it's all peaceful and fine. Rosie is going out then, with her family, to some do or other connected with their church. They ask me to go, but I do not feel ready to be completely reformed as yet, so I go back indoors to grub and telly.

Later, Mark comes in, and he's in a heck of a good mood, he's got the chance of a job, working for this car firm. He's pretty sure that he'll get it.

"I'll see you're all right, kid," he says, putting his hand upon my shoulder, with huge matiness. "I didn't mean what I said the other night. I was legless. You don't have to take any notice of me when I'm legless. I didn't mean what I said about the little rat. I wouldn't harm your little rat. You know better than that. Let's look at the little fellow. I brought somethin' special for him."

He brings a small pork pie out of his pocket.

"For Boris Karloff, the rat," he says.

I don't know what to do, haven't a clue.

"Go on. Fetch him. What's the matter?"

After a bit I manage to say,

"He's gone."

"Gone? Gone where? What d'ye mean? What you done with the little rat?"

"Nuthin'. Just gone, that's all."

"You mean he's lost?"

"Yeh. Ye . . . eh. Somethin' like that."

"Hey, what's the matter with you? Why you like that?"

"Like what?"

"You're telling lies."

He's got me, by now, shaking me. He's grown very strong since we used to scrap.

"Tell me what you done with it?"

Suddenly he flings me against the door and rushes

down the cellar. I pick myself up and start to move fast out of the house, but for once he is on the ball and he drags me away from the front door.

"You taken them all away. All the little creatures. Don't you trust me? Your own brother?"

"You said about vivisection."

It's difficult to say 'cos he's holding me up against the wall, his head on a level with mine, and he's banging my head back against it, feet swinging off the ground.

"You know I didn't mean it? Didn'ja?"

"No."

"And you took 'em away. Where?"

I don't answer. He shakes my head for me.

"You took them to that girl, didn'ja?"

I don't answer.

"Well, we'll soon find out."

He marches me next door, but it's locked, for the Lees are out, at church, singing and praying. For me, Rosie. I'm the one that needs your prayer, Rosie.

He's in a rage now.

"I'll break the bloody door in."

And for a moment he lets me go, so that he can shove his weight at it.

"I won't have our creatures in there!"

This time I'm not slow. I'm gone, at the speed of light, faster than fast. But where can I go, till he's calmed down and Mum's home again?

And so I come to school, the school I used to hate, before Rosie came, and it feels like home, like what was it Sir taught us about? I know. Sanctuary. I'm over the railings, and down behind the dustbins as Mark rushes on. I wait and watch, catching my breath. Mouse and

Peter Tawnay and Rod Gillott have pulled up on their motor bikes, under the lamplight. They are talking, turning, going back to our house, probably. I can't go back, yet. I move away, walk round the school building, looking for a way in. It will be warm inside. Safe. There must be a way in. Then he won't find me. The toilet window is open by one of the cloakrooms. Not very far open, but it will do. I pull myself up and I'm inside. It's pitch dark. If I can get to my classroom, I'll be all right. I know where there are some candles, and Sir has some matches in his desk. I don't want to put the lights on. I make my way through the unlit school. It's a good thing I know it so well.

I have been sitting by the mouse cage, with my candle, and chewing some gum I kept in reserve away from Rosie for some minutes before I remember that headless lady, the Saint.

Chapter 14

Keep in, keep in, wherever you are,
The rats and mice are at your door.

If I get out of this lot, I'll be good for ever, oh, God, I say to the flickering candle and the little mice. I'll go to church with Rosie, and I'll stop tormenting Heather, and I'll write to Dad, and I'll leave JJ alone. If they want me still, I'll even join the Team, well, perhaps. But I'll definitely give up watching horror films. In fact I never want to see a horror film again as long as I live, which won't be very long the way my heart's pounding now.

What's that?

That. That noise. That kind of low moaning noise.

It seems to be coming from the direction of the cellar. Don't think about the cellar, Gowie Corby. That's when all this haunting stuff started. Suppose, just suppose she came out from down there, in her long white gown stained with blood, and her head dripping, oh, no, no, no don't think about it, or the skeletons rattling.

The thing to do is to get out of here, fast.

But, but, wait a minute, suppose, just suppose, the school is changing, altering while I am here, inside, trapped inside, changing to that school of older times, the one the cleaner talked about and like that time you came back with Rosie and *couldn't find the door*. Oh, no, not that. I'd almost rather have the headless saint, at least saints are supposed to be good, aren't they, whereas old schools could be filled with the wickedness of kids like me . . . no. No, I daren't go. I'll stay here a minute with the mice and the candle and . . . and . . . ROSIE'S PRAYER.

God Save the Children, especially this one, please. Rosie, think about me wherever you are. Save the children, every one. Yes, that includes me.

The noise has stopped. That's better. Come on, Corby. You're supposed to have guts. What a laugh. You've less guts than a filletted kipper, crouching here too scared to go back to Rosie's house, just 'cos of a few old stupid yarns from some thickies.

That's better. Chew away at the old gum. It's just school, nothing strange about it, you've known it all your life. Just take the candle, get out and go home. There aren't any ghosts. Oh, no? I've never been sure whether there were or not. Whatever that noise was, probably the wind, Rosie's prayer sent it away. Right. Off we go.

Another noise, oh, there's another noise, a moaning again, only different, no, no, I can't bear it, it seems to be saying my name, you don't think it's come to get me, do you, listen, listen, it's saying, Gowie, Gowie Corby, and, it can't be, Count Dracula, are you there?

"ROSIE!"

"Count Dracula!"

"My favourite ghoul."

"He came looking for you, just as we were coming back from church, and he was angry and I guessed you'd run away somewhere and I had to find out where, and I went to the Chinese takeaway, to see if you were there for a bit, and then I went to the Kasbah and Simon hadn't seen you, nor Darren, and when I came back past school, I saw this tiny, little light..." she stops for breath, and I can get a word in edgeways....

"Did you get in through the toilet window?"

"Sure."
"Let's get out the same way, then."
"You're not gonna stay for the dare?"
"No way."

"Yeh, it is kinda spooky in here. Can't we put a light on for a minute?

"No, just let's get out."

"You scared?"

"Me? Never."

"Liar. Let's go, then. You can come on along to our house till Mark's cooled off a little."

It's funny how brave you can be when there's two of you. I am whistling a bit, and thinking about grub and watching telly after all the excitement of mad Mark and haunted schools. Rosie climbs on to a chair to reach the window.

"Shh," she whispers. "There's someone out there. Get back. It's your brother and Mouseface, and some others."

"Oh, no. That's all we need."

Back we creep to the classroom, which I barely seem to have left all day. For an empty building this school is remarkably busy, tonight.

"Under the work bench. They're coming this way."

The tinkle of broken glass indicates that they've found the window a bit small for them.

We bang our heads, shooting under the bench between two craft bins.

"The candle," hisses Rosie. We blow it out.

Heavy boots, clinking bottles and lighted matches approach.

"I'm sure the little beast must've come in here," says my loving brother.

"Whassit matter? Have a drink and stop being so bloomin' miserable."

It sounds as if Mouse has been on the bottle for some

time. I am not happy. Mouse is noted for some pretty habits when he's in the mood. Rosie and I crouch down as still as dead wombats, only she is trembling every now and then in sort of waves.

Mark is still muttering about what he will do to me when he finds me, but Mouse and Peter are walking round the room, looking at pictures and throwing dead matches all over the floor. Gillott has a torch and is waving it about.

"Remember when we was in here with old Potty Barnes?"

"The old devil. Used to hit me with a slipper."

"I liked 'im," says Peter Tawnay. "Eh, look 'ere, Mouse, at this painting. Ain't bad."

"Load of old rubbish." Mouse tears it off the wall.

"You shouldn't do that."

"I do what I like. See?"

"Nice cassette player here."

My brother has found it. It should have been put away. He'll never keep his hands off it. He hasn't.

"I'll just have this one small thing. Better one than mine. They won't miss it. Besides, it's too good for the kids. Remember how we used to smash things up, eh, Mouse?"

They haven't changed much either, from the way that Mouse is pulling out all the drawers of the teacher's desk and throwing them on the floor. Above the noise, Peter and Rod are still wandering down Memory Lane.

"I wonder what happened to old Lily Pond? Remember when she kept you in till half-past four and your Dad came?"

"Yeah. He didn't 'alf pitch into 'er."

All this time matches are being lit and thrown down.

"It's like a nightmare," murmurs Rosie.

"Sh." They don't hear. Mouse is tearing all the pictures off the walls.

"What a load of old crap," he says, reading out Rosie's prayer.

"My brother wants beating, not saving," says Mark.

Mouse sets fire to Rosie's poem and the flame lights up the room.

"That's pretty," he says. "Let's set the school on fire."

"Eh, cool it, Mouse," says Mark. "We'll have the fuzz 'ere."

Rosie beside me has gone even more tense and, suddenly, she leaps out into the middle of the vandalised room, and stands there, black and quite terrible, her eyes huge and white and shining. She points to them in turn, Mark and Mouse, Rod and Peter. Her finger shakes, but with, I see, anger, not fear. It's me who's afraid. I'm terrified. She doesn't know what they're like, and slowly, reluctantly, I stand up behind, just to be there to pick up the bits, and because she is my friend, even if I'm not much of a friend, and with no guts at all.

"*You Nasty Nerks*," she says, and she is not shouting, but there is complete silence in the room. "You come in here, and you spoil our school and our work, and you frighten our mouses, and you are drunk and horrible. You will *not* set fire to our school—" and as if obeying, the paper and the matches burn out at that moment, leaving us with the light of Gillott's torch.

"—and you will go home now and think how to make the world a good place, not a bad one."

128

And behind me I hear another noise, I think I am the only one who has, and Thank Heaven for the Fuzz, which I have never said before, because it has just dawned on Mouse that Rosie is only a black girl, not a spirit or a ghost, and the surprise and fear are wearing off, and he is moving towards her slowly, which is a thing I do not want to see, not at all, no, thank you.

"Quick. Move. The Fuzz," I say and grab Rosie's arm.

I don't care where the others go, though a part of me that doesn't hate Mark at all hopes he's got enough sense to scram, or he'll be for it, but I know where I'm going and Rosie's going with me, Headless Ghost or not. Dear Lord Above Save us from Mark, Mouse, the Fuzz and all Headless Women, Saints or otherwise. And I head for the broom cupboard in the corridor outside our room, and the new way leading to the dreaded cellar, where it seems a strong doom has been leading me all evening despite the fact that I don't want to go there at all. We leap into the cupboard still full of carpet sweepers, vacuum cleaners, mop, buckets, Vim, paper towels and bog rolls. I try to shut the door, but am stopped by the bodies of Mark, Mouse, Peter and Rod (old Uncle Tom Cobley and all) coming up behind in the absolute pitch-blackness.

"Shut the door," I grunt. Several dozen bog rolls descend from the shelf above us, and somebody falls over a broom. The door closes.

"Put the torch on a minute, and I'll open the other door."

Outside feet are walking about, investigating the

damage in our classroom, no doubt. I open the new door at the back of the cupboard, a sliding one, and we are through.

"Close it up," I say, "and they'll never find us, 'cos it still looks as if it's only a cupboard."

We are on the other side, sighs of relief as we creep quietly along the corridor and down the new cellar steps. Round into the corner hidden by the same steps and there we are. We fall down in a heap. I'm still holding Rosie, but she is next to Mouse on her other side, and Mark is beside me and no one would ever guess we'd ever said a harsh word to each other.

"You all right, kid?" he says.

Amazing what danger can do!

" 'United by the enemy' or 'The Fuzz made us Friends'," I think.

"How long do we have to sit here?" asks Peter.

"Till they go away, stupid," Mouse answers.

"I've been down here before. There's another door leading to the playground. Let's try it."

But it's locked and though Mark, the biggest of us, puts his shoulder to it, it won't budge. He goes away and listens for a bit.

"They're still here," he says.

All of a sudden I feel very tired. I lean back against the wall.

"You're a funny kid," says Mouse, lighting a cigarette which glows in the dark. Peter has put out his torch to save the battery.

"Who is?" asks Rosie.

"You. Coming out like that and tellin' us off. I like that. You did what was right. We shouldn't have been

130

mucking up the old place. Some of the teachers was very nice. Rotten job teaching us little devils."

"I didn't take the cassette player," says Mark.

I don't say that was because he was too busy running away, I feel too knackered. Silence falls on us as we sit there waiting till we can get out of the dark cellar. I push my hands into the bottom of my pockets and the left one finds something, what Rosie had called that little ole key. That seems like something out of the past, long ago, when I imagined I could work things by wishing on the key. Being walloped by Sir had finished that off. I yawn away in the dark, still holding the key. Now I am feeling sleepy, which is strange when you think of it, for I wouldn't have thought it possible to feel sleepy in that dark, uncomfortable cellar, with the police investigating up above and trouble if they find us, but I do. I feel as if I could sleep on a clothes line. Nothing matters at all, I'm not scared. I feel as if I'm safe with friends, and everything's far away and remote. And I don't know if I'm dreaming or not, but in the furthest, darkest corner of the cellar shines a soft light, a gentle glow, and just for a moment I see something that changes to someone who has long fair hair, wearing a white gown, and she smiles very sweetly at me so that I feel quite strange, and I see that she has her head on safely, and that's a good thing, I say, and blimey, I am awake and she's gone, leaving only a memory of some-one, someone else but familiar.

"Yes, they have gone," says my brother Mark, com-ing down the steps. "It's all clear. We can 'oppit, now."

We go back through the broom cupboard, and the sad, untidy classroom. Then, very cautiously, through the broken window, lest they are waiting for us. But it's all quiet. We can go home and sleep.

Walking along, holding Rosie with one hand and the little ole key with the other, I feel as if I'm walking in a world where time is measureless. But Rosie giggles.

"The trouble is," she says, "you'll never be able to say you did spend a night in school, after all, because if you do, well, there will be trouble."

"I shall just tell JJ he's right and I'm chicken," I yawn. "That'll make him happy."

At last I am in bed. Only, before I drop in Mark puts his head round the door.

"You can bring the little rats back. I shan't do anything to them. And I won't tell Mum." And, "Rosie's all right. I don't mind if you're mates."

Tomorrow we'll have to clean up for Sir, but then, tomorrow is a whole new day.

Chapter 15

Ittle ottle
Black bottle
Ittle ottle OUT.

It's morning. I've been going round the school with a notice from Sir, and in every class all the kiddiwinkies are working away at their Maths or their English or whatever it is and a great peace lies over all. In our class Darren is scribbling frantically like the genius he is, and Rosie is covering half a page with a word as she goes. Heather is happy for once. Her face reminds me of someone, no, not a hippo, but I can't remember who or what.

What a beautiful, peaceful day.

Why not today?

Seems like the right moment. While the school is so quiet, as it is now.

So I get up to sharpen a pencil, and just open the cage-door one tiny, little fraction. Oh, frabjous day. We did that poem, yesterday. I like it. Soon, now, soon.

Wait for it.

Eight minutes later a cry goes up.

"Sir, the mice are escaping!"

Tom, Jerry and their ten children have come out of

133

the cage and got down the table and are now spreading to all four corners of this classroom. Which hasn't any door, because of open planning.

On and on they run through that quiet working school, all the lovely little beasties. And as they go, children are standing up, forgetting their books, shrieking, screeching, running after them, trying to catch them, dropping tupperware containers on them hopefully, throwing hats, running, shouting as the twelve mice speed on and on in all directions through the school.

I sit back and smile in delight. Only, watching me, is Sir, Mr. Merchant, Sir.

"Gowie Corby," he is saying. "Gowie Corby. I don't trust that smirk on your unlovely countenance. You let them out, didn't you?"

I watch Heather fall flat on her face as she tries to stop one running under the table, and this is a lovely sight.

"Me, Sir? Never, Sir. How can you possibly think such a thing?"

And the pandemonium in the school grows louder and louder and LOUDER.

Epilogue

"Did they catch all the mice safely?"

"Yes, but it took all morning. It was great."

"And did the police find out who broke into school?"

"No, fortunately for us."

"What happened to Rosie, next?"

"She stayed in England for quite a while and we went to the Comprehensive together. Then she went away, but we stayed friends."

"She didn't fancy marrying you, though, Dad," says the second one.

"Well, she couldn't just look after Dad, when she's got all those children to take care of," says the youngest, licking the jam spoon.

"Shut up, Rosie Corby," says the second. "You've got too much to say, just because you're the only girl and the pet."

"That's enough," says their father.

"Tell me one thing, Dad," asks the third child, the quiet one.

"One more, then that's it."

"Who was it that that ghost, that lady in the cellar, reminded you of? It couldn't have been Rosie, because she's black and the lady ghost had long fair hair, and it wasn't your teacher 'cos she was dark, and it couldn't have been Gran, it just couldn't."

135

"Why, your mother, of course. That's why I married her."

"Rubbish. You did no such thing. I married you, Gowie Corby," says Heather, helping herself to another cup of coffee.